WORK
pouse

I'm His
FROM NINE TO FIVE

A LOVE@WORK SERIES NOVEL

PAX SINCLAIR

ISBN: 978-1-7336445-5-6 (Print Edition)
ASIN: B08X2ZXC9J (ebook Edition)

Printed and bound in the United States of America
First printing February 2021

Red Kettle Ink

Published by Red Kettle Ink
2010 El Camino Real #1151
Santa Clara, CA 95050

www.paxsinclair.com

Book Cover by Uniquely Tailored
www.uniquelytailored.com

Acknowledgments

I want to thank my wonderful beta team.
I don't know where I'd be without your guidance.
Thanks Ash, Maureen, Lucie, Jeanie and Latoya.

TABLE OF CONTENTS

Knock Knock

NOVEMBER - ELECTION NIGHT

Cold shoots up through my knees from the hard tile floor. I try not to breathe in too deeply to avoid the stench. It's really the not-too-clean ground that has me worried as I adjust to the unforgiving surface.

I'm in an airless bathroom paying homage to the porcelain throne, throwing up cocktail weenies and chardonnay, wishing this night had turned out differently.

"Chloe!" she calls between the sounds of her fist beating the door.

A slight headache is beginning as I pull my face away from the toilet and groan. The pounding is like a reverberating base. I grasp the bowl to push up, but I can't help it; I fall back on my knees and retch again.

"Are you alright? What's got you so spooked?"

I hit the handle and watch my stomach's contents swirl down and away. My mouth tastes foul and bile burns my throat, reminding me I'm still not under control. I take a shaky breath and wipe my mouth with the back of my hand, then twist my dark hair away from my shoulders to cool the dampness on my brow. God, it's hot in here.

"I'm fine," I call back and slowly get to my feet.

"You're not fine. I can hear you throwing up from here. Let me in."

More pounding.

My hand rests on the wall to steady myself, while I pull the door open to a horrified Kellis, her fist poised to break down the door. Kurt is behind her, attempting to peer over her shoulder. She exchanges a glance with my concerned brother-in-law and he leaves without a word. She walks in, locking the door behind her.

"You look like shit," she says, advancing to the sink to reach for a paper towel, and taps the faucet. "Do you think you have food poisoning?"

I move to the second sink, wash my hands, then cup my palm for water to rinse my mouth. I lean over the running faucet exhausted; my stomach feels like it's inside out from food spewing out of me. "I'm not sick," I mumble.

She offers me a moistened towel. "Here, wipe your face, then tell me why you ran in here after Councilman Peterson gave his concession speech."

I take the offered towel, wipe half my makeup off, and discard it in the trash. "According to all the polling data," I say in an exhale, "Peterson should have easily won his race."

My sister digs into her purse, pulls out her makeup bag, and hands it to me. "Here, use this to repair the damage. Although my lipstick is a lot brighter than you're used to." She rinses her hands while she speaks to me through the mirror. "What's the deal? Sometimes politicians lose, and I didn't think you were that fond of your boss."

I wet another towel to get the rest of my makeup off. "Peterson was alright; it was like working for my grandfather." I'm feeling better while I wick the last bit of foundation off my face. "I'm not heartbroken about his leaving. He told me this would be his last term. I'm worried about the person who's taking his council seat."

Kellis' reflection says she doesn't have a clue what I'm talking about. She's been living in Munich with her new husband and is expecting their first child. They arrived earlier today because she convinced her husband, the CEO of Drachen Technology, to temporarily move back to Silicon Valley to be close to our family when she gives birth. So, she doesn't have a notion about local politics.

The eyeliner and lipstick I apply are enough to get through the hotel if I see anyone from the campaign. "Let's get out of here and I'll show you why I'm upset."

Kurt sits at our abandoned table with empty glasses and plates of half-eaten food. Someone must have released the balloons and confetti that were tacked to the ceiling to celebrate a victory that never came. He looks like the last guest at a New Year's Eve celebration.

The hotel crew is doing their best to clean around his big, imposing form. He's a modern version of a brooding romantic figure like Rochester in *Jane Eyre* with his short blond hair bordering on a military style and crystal-blue eyes that miss nothing. He's an 'A' type and needs a better social filter, but he's a big sweetie and loves my sister. He stands, towering over me, his brows knit together. "Are you alright, Chloe?"

I beam at him, happy that two of my favorite people are back in my life. "I'm better now. Something didn't agree with my stomach, that's all." I grab my purse and jacket he was guarding. "I didn't drive here; can I ride with you guys?"

We walk through the door. I flip on lights, grateful the cleaner has been here and the house looks tidy. It's good to have Kellis back living with me, even if Kurt is with her. The three of us spent a lot of mornings in our kitchen when Kurt first came to the US from Germany when he lived next door.

"Have a seat," I say, motioning them to the couch. "I'm sure I can find the new councilman's acceptance speech on the news." I press the remote, surfing the stations, until I settle on channel two. The ten o'clock news team is calling the city races. I turn the volume up when the female anchor gets to San Pacitas.

"Today, we witnessed a stunning defeat of Councilman Alfred Peterson, a city councilman who has represented District 5 for the last fifteen years. The upset came from a political newcomer and ex-Silicon Valley tech mogul Jaxson Bennett."

Kellis gapes when she sees Jaxson at the podium, standing with his excited supporters crowding the stage. A full battery of press jostles for position below the dais, hanging on his every word. I click off the TV.

Kellis glances over at me. "That's not...it can't be the same Jaxson Bennett from Anselm Prep."

I slump into a chair. "Yeah, that's him."

"Who's Jaxson Bennett?" Kurt's bewildered voice is barely audible.

Kellis notices her puzzled spouse. "Sweetheart, would you get me an orange juice?"

A worried Kurt bounces to his feet, looking down at his wife. "I will. Are you feeling alright, Schatz?"

I have to stifle a laugh when I hear him call her his treasure in German. It's funny to see them now, but it was WWIII around here before they realized they were meant for each other. Kurt fell in love first; it just took me convincing my stubborn sister he was Mr. Right.

"I'm fine," Kellis says, in her sweet, calming voice she's been using when she speaks to Kurt. I wonder how she holds it together sometimes. "I'm just a little thirsty." He practically jogs out of the room to do her bidding.

She leans toward me. "Start talking."

Cabinets are banging, but I still crane my neck to see if Kurt is in the kitchen, just to make sure he doesn't hear us, then sit beside Kellis on the couch.

"There's nothing to tell. You know Jax came back to the Valley after graduating from Princeton. He opened a data-mining company using some of his trust fund money with a few of his buddies and entered the billionaire boys club a few years later." All noise stops from the kitchen and I lower my voice. "We're not in the same social circles, so I was never in danger of running into him."

Kurt returns, holding a tray with two glasses, a pitcher of juice, plates, napkins, and a bowl of carrot sticks. Kellis is in the early months of her pregnancy; Lord help us when she starts looking like Lady Madonna. Kurt will probably have her hermetically sealed until the baby arrives.

He places the tray on the coffee table and kisses his wife on the top of her head. "Drink your orange juice," he instructs. "The only healthy thing I found for you to eat were carrots." He turns to me. "Chloe, I'll help you make a grocery list tomorrow."

I nod, indulging my overprotective brother-in-law.

He looks at her critically. "Schatz, don't you think you should have your feet up?"

"I'm fine, Kurt, don't fuss. You said you had to return some calls. Why don't you do that now and let us talk? It will take your mind off of me for a while."

He's reluctant. "Okay, if you think I'm hovering."

"Oh, no, never you." I smile up at him."

He points an accusing finger at me. "We're going to Whole Foods tomorrow." Then he turns to stride out of the room.

"I look forward to it," I shout at his back.

Kellis pours a glass and hands it to me. "Be sure you have some of these carrot sticks; I'm betting he's counted them. Why is Jax in politics?"

I pull out a magazine from under a stack of books on the table and place it on her lap. She puts her glass down to retrieve it. Jaxson Bennett's rich-guy good looks dominate the cover of *Silicon Valley Today*. "The interview is on page twenty-five," I say.

Kellis runs a finger over the worn cover. "This magazine is dated over a year ago."

"Yeah, so?"

She flips through the pages, looking for the article. "This is a real magazine; most people read their news on a device."

I shrug. "What can I say? I like the feel of glossy paper in my hands."

Kellis is silent while she reads, then turns a page. "Most of what he's saying in this article is pretty much political speak. That he wants to serve the community and make a positive impact. I see here he's still single," she teases in a sing-song voice.

I shake my head, indicating that she's missing the point. "When I saw that article, I called around to find out if his bid for the seat had any merit or if he was just doing it to boost his public profile. Every pollster, every political writer I spoke to said he didn't have a chance to unseat Peterson."

"How do you think Jaxson managed it?"

"My guess is that he threw a lot of money at it and because Peterson was the incumbent, he didn't take Jax or his own campaign seriously."

"Are you sure you're going to be assigned to Jaxson?"

"He's replacing the councilman I work for...I'm positive. I can ask Arlene, my supervisor, to switch me to another councilmember. But I know she's not going to approve my request. They're not going to chance a newbie working with a high-profiled politician. I'll show him how the system works, but I'm also tasked with keeping him out of trouble, and with his reputation it might be difficult."

Kellis pushes the magazine back on the table. "When does he assume his new position?"

I fish a carrot stick out of the bowl. "The swearing-in ceremony will be after the councilmembers are officially certified. I think it's scheduled for the first week in January. The day after the swearing-in, the new members will attend an orientation. That day or the next, he'll meet me and the rest of his staff."

"After all this time, what are you going to say to him?"

I shrug. I've got to convince her that Jax is no big deal. "I haven't seen him since my first quarter at SCU. We were together for a few weeks until he was accepted into Princeton and vanished."

Kellis reaches for my hand and I grasp it, happy for our sister bond. We've always had each other's back no matter what's been thrown at us.

"Don't worry, little sister," I say as I squeeze her hand, "everything will work out. Jax and I will probably have coffee together and have a good laugh."

This doesn't sit well with her. She's giving me a glimpse of what's in store for her kid. "Really, Chloe? It took you a long time to get over Jaxson, even though you dated for a short period and he unceremoniously dumped you after that. What is there to laugh about?"

I won't admit to my sister that I still think about him. That's not weird…people do that. I haven't done it for a while, but I've driven by his house hoping to catch a glimpse of him. I can't show her the stack of articles I've collected about him over the years; she'd probably drive me to a therapist.

"After the night you spent together, you told me he was the love of your life. Chloe, at least try to get some closure."

I wave the suggestion away. Usually, I'm the one giving out advice. Kellis is the head of a thriving staffing firm married to Kurt, a CEO of a multinational company, and they've got a baby on the way. I'm a legislative analyst for a councilman in local city government. That proves I give great advice to everyone else.

"That was years ago. I've moved on. We're both adults and we'll handle it like adults."

Kellis crunches a carrot stick, then points the end at me. "Yeah, throwing up in the bathroom after you find out Jaxson Bennett is going to be your boss is real adult."

2

Traffic Patterns

JANUARY - CITY COUNCIL SWEARING-IN DAY

My morning drive to work is the best predictor of how the day will go. Today is the swearing-in of the new councilmembers for the city of San Pacitas. Jaxson Bennett, the only man I can't seem to leave in the past, will take public office today. I haven't seen him in years and I'm still crushed by the way he ended our relationship, so today, my drive can't tell me what I already know.

The red light blinks green, preventing me from making a right turn ahead of ongoing traffic. Instead, I inch my way over three lanes of cars that are whizzing down the expressway to get to the freeway on-ramp. After I exit the highway to take city streets, I catch every red light. More grief, when I sit at my last traffic light, a left-hand turn into a crowded intersection. City Hall is three blocks on the right after this turn. Every time I'm caught by this light, I swear

I'm going to talk to the head of Traffic Control and asked them to recalibrate the lights at this intersection.

Sitting in the turning lane, about fifteen cars back, I estimate it'll take three signal rotations before I can turn on the green arrow. I turn down the news I'm not listening to and reach in my bag. I apply lipstick, the one I pinched from Kellis. I pout at the rearview mirror, admiring the bright-pink shade on my lips. The cars ahead aren't moving, but three people, two men and a woman, are walking along the street divider. They're all dressed in firefighter's bottoms, suspenders, a blue T-shirt, and a firefighter's helmet. The men are holding a tall boot, soliciting donations.

The fire department is doing a series of fundraising events for a new fire station/training center. The city had allocated money for the project until the drought and unexpected fires in the hills diverted some of the money to other services. The shortfall forced the fire department to do their own fundraising for their much-needed projects.

I find my wallet and pull three ones, two fives, a ten, and two twenty-dollar bills and dump them in the cupholder, satisfied I've got enough for a reasonable donation. I relax and wait my turn while the two men work the cars. It looks like they've been doing this for a while, enough to know how long to spend at each vehicle.

The female stands a distance away on the road divider with something that looks like folders in her hands.

The guys could be the poster boys for firefighter recruiting. The rangy blond looks like an eager rookie, with a guileless, open grin. He's a little shorter than the tall, dark-haired bruiser that's working with him. I can't see his face while he's in conversation with someone one car ahead of me. As soon as he steps away, a manicured hand with a smattering of gold bracelets attached flies out of the car window, motioning him to come back. He listens for a few moments, then shakes his head and gestures to the cars. When he manages to step away, his curious gaze settles on me. Our eyes lock in an eerie moment of recognition that tugs at something primal inside me, but it's the small shiver that glides through my body that has me worried. I've never seen this man before. Because I sure as hell would have remembered that face and this feeling. This isn't the first time I've had a strong response to a man. The last time I had this same reaction, it didn't end in my favor. I redirect my gaze down the road to pretend something else has caught my interest, to get myself in control and wonder why this happened.

The light changes and the guys step back to watch the cars reposition. I can't stop looking at him as I move forward. Firefighters here are hot-looking, and I'm not exaggerating. I don't know who hires the male applicants for the fire stations in San Pacitas, but I'm positive they must have a big handsome requirement listed in the job description.

Two cars make the light on this short rotation. That means another added rotation until I can make it through. I'd be annoyed at my luck if it wasn't for the firefighter eye-candy show.

The blond firefighter is approaching my car with his boot and a ready smile for a donation. I pick out the two fives and the ones. That's more than enough money for a fundraiser. It doesn't look like I'm going to talk to the dark-haired hottie; he's going to pass me by.

When the dark-haired firefighter is done with his car, he jogs up to the determined blond, taps the guy on the shoulder, and points to the car behind me.

I snatch up a few more bills. It's for a good cause and I don't want to appear cheap, at least not to this guy.

My heart picks up as he saunters toward me like time has slowed, allowing me to observe a firefighter's recruiting poster come to life. Real time resumes when he casually anchors himself against my car, sliding his arm along the top of the window and leaning in. "Care to donate to a good cause like your fellow commuters? He throws his hand out to include the captive drivers in front of me. "We're out here soliciting donations for a new firehouse/training station."

He's drawing me in with his perpetual smile, although this guy has it honed as a wicked grin, like he's up to something and you're hoping it might include you. "Yes," is all I say.

He pushes his helmet back, releasing a tousled black lock, thinking God knows what with that spark of mischief in his ink-blue eyes. He holds the tall rubber boot up like an offering. I look at it and draw a blank.

"Your donation, Miss?"

I've been staring at him like I'm watching a snake charmer. "Oh, right." I thrust my hand into the cupholder, scoop out the rest of my bills, and throw it all in. His eyes widen as my donation rains into the tall boot. He must be impressed, because I get a genuine smile for my efforts that has my heart beating a manic pace that I'm afraid won't stop.

He places the boot on the ground and crouches to eye level with me. I inhale male, cold smoky air and soap that seems to calm my overworked heart. If I'm around him for much longer, I could eliminate aerobics for today.

"Would you be interested in buying a fireman's calendar? Station 38 has put one together. A lot of us are firehouse cooks. There's a firefighter cook profiled each month with their favorite recipe. I'm featured this month."

Again, with a grin that says, *I'm a freakin hottie, want to do something about it?* He's enough of an incentive to buy the calendar, if he'll throw in his T-shirt as part of the deal and rip it off while I watch.

"Sure, anything to support our firefighters." I smile at him. "How much is the calendar?"

He dims his smile and moves in for the sell. "If you think about it, it's really a cookbook with twelve recipes and a few bonus dishes added at the end. Some other guys at the station wanted to include their moms' recipes. It's $30, but all the proceeds go to the fire station fund."

The light turns green and more cars move ahead. The guy pushes to his full height and keeps pace as I roll the car forward, then stop. I realize I've nothing left; I've given him all my cash.

"Chelsea," he yells over his shoulder, "can you hand me one of those calendars?" The female firefighter jogs over and gives him an oversize poster. "Here," he says, "this has some of our best recipes. They've been tested; it's not easy pleasing a bunch of hungry firefighters."

The big, glossy wall calendar has a rendering of the new fire facility on the cover. I hazard a peek over the calendar into his eyes and heat rises in some uncomfortable places. I check the traffic ahead; I figure the light is about to change. "I'm sorry, but I have no more cash with me."

His lips press into a disappointed line. He tilts his chin down, looking into the car. I'm about to reach for my purse to show him the empty wallet.

"This parking sticker on your dashboard says you're a city employee. I can go over to your office after we're done and collect the money from you."

I shake my head. He's got more important things to do than to run after thirty bucks. I try to hand the calendar back to him. "I don't want you to do that; it seems like an imposition."

I didn't want to take a trip to the ATM. I'd have to walk about four blocks and I wouldn't have the time today. Then I remember I have about sixty dollars in my secret emergency cash box sitting in my desk drawer.

He's pinning me with his blue eyes and faint grin. "No imposition. It's for a good cause. I've got to go to the city to drop off the donations to the Accounting department."

The green light changes and I need to move forward, but I hesitate. He taps the car's hood and backs away. The vehicle in front is already two car lengths away. I toss the calendar onto the passenger seat. "Okay, you can come by my office," I say as the car rolls forward. The cars in back are honking.

Before I'm able to move much further, he yells, "What's your name?"

"Chloe," I yell back, but I'm not sure if he heard me. I just make the light.

City Hall resembles an industrious beehive anticipating the swearing-in ceremony a few hours away. I'll be in the back of the council chambers watching as Jax is sworn in to begin his term. Every time I think about it, my stomach does tiny somersaults of worry. Nothing to do but to ignore the persistent flutter until I have a chance to speak to him.

Dominica, an analyst with Councilmember Turner and my favorite work friend, pokes her head into my office. "Are you ready for the changing of the guard?" She's already slipping inside my office.

I give her a half shrug. "I'm ready. This isn't our first and hopefully not our last swearing-in ceremony."

Her slender frame lands in the chair in front of my desk. "Do you believe it? This is the largest turnover of councilmembers we've seen in decades. The other councilmembers up for reelection in the next cycle are all nervous as hell. They think the mood of the districts has changed."

"That seems to be the general consensus," I say, considering, "but my political sense doesn't agree. I think the councilmembers that were voted out were close to retirement. I just think the other party saw an opportunity to retire them earlier and win a seat."

Dominica throws a wary glance at the door, then moves her

attention back to me. I'm used to her excessive need for caution; Dominica can't live without drama.

"I'm just glad Cheryl kept her seat," she says in a stage whisper. "You know she can be a witch on wheels, and it's taken me all this time to break her in. If I had to start over with someone else, I don't know what I'd do..." Her dark eyes blink, realizing what she just said, then she rushes out with an apology. "Hey, I'm sorry. I forgot Peterson lost his race."

I swivel in my old chair; the loud creak breaks the silence as I consider what she said. Aides work so closely with their councilmembers, sometimes it's hard to know where you end and they begin. "Don't worry about it. He told me this would be his last term," I sigh. "I was expecting to work with someone new, just not so soon."

"I didn't need to point it out." Her nails make impatient taps on the armrest. "Did you hear about the latest rumor?"

My ears prick up. Now we're getting to the reason for her visit. "Rumor about what?" I don't want to appear too eager or she'll take her time with the gossip. "There are always rumors flying around this place, Dom, you need to be more specific."

The corner of her mouth quirks up. She's happy that she has something to taunt me with until I'm begging her to tell me.

"That proves you haven't heard this big juicy bit of gossip or you wouldn't be sitting in your seat so calm. Unless you're a better poker player than I thought."

It must be really good if she's torturing me before the reveal. Dominica has a vast, unmatched city network with the most accurate dirt on everyone. "Spill it. Obviously, you think it's something that I'd be interested in."

"Girlfriend," she says, almost bursting, "you especially will be interested in this news." Her hair cascades in a long black shiny sheath when she leans forward, elbows on my desk. "I've just heard that Rita is stepping down and they're going to need a new Assistant City

Manager. HR doesn't even know about it."

I rear back into my chair, looking at Dominica's satisfied face that she got this level of surprise from her news. Even before I started here as an intern, my goal has been to be City Manager. If the assistant position is opening up, I'm going for it. Today of all days, I needed to hear some good news. "Thanks for letting me know. I owe you big for this, "I say.

She waves the gratitude away. "We're friends; you'd do the same for me…right?"

"Right."

She pulls out her phone and frowns at it. "I've got to brief Cheryl on today's agenda. I'll see you at the swearing-in." She gets up, adjusts her skirt, then tosses her hair back. "They should post the position within the week. I suggest when you find out the essay questions on the application that you work on them as soon as possible. You know they prefer a thesis. I suspect if it's long enough, they'll stop reading after a page and admire your diligence."

"I'd almost forgotten…thanks for the advice."

Dominica hesitates before heading for the door. "This isn't going to be easy." Her brows draw together. "You know how city government works. They like to hire from within. The councilmembers will decide who takes that position. Monica has influence over most of them, and she might have someone else in mind."

3

Hammer Time

Steam rises from my mug, along with the aroma of French roast. It seems strange not to begin my day in Councilman Peterson's office to discuss the day's agenda. A few days ago, Peterson and I met for a long-overdue dinner. He wanted to thank me for my support and to give me advice on how to navigate the man who's taking his seat.

There's no official work until I meet with Councilman Bennett. The desk clock says I've got time before the swearing-in ceremony to hang the firefighter's calendar sitting on my desk. It might distract me, take my mind off of seeing Jax today.

My office is no bigger than a large storage closet. It's been my office home for the last five years, enough time to have a memory wall covered with pictures to the ceiling. I rummage in my top drawer for a few nails, then drag a chair over to the wall, take off my heels, but keep one in case I need a hammer. Stepping up, I place my shoe on the tall shelf next to me and remove a few pictures. When

I've cleared a space, there's a problem pulling out a nail from the wall. Grabbing my shoe, I try to tap the nail loose when knocking on my door distracts me.

"Ms. Ivarsson?"

"Come in," I call out, still focused on the task.

Samir, a tall, gangling intern, steps into the office with a box tucked under his arm.

"We found this in Councilman Peterson's office. We thought you might know how to get it to him?"

I'm looking down at his expectant face, considering the request. "Yeah, I can deliver it to him." I point with my shoe and say, "Just leave it over there in the corner. Have you seen Councilman-Elect Bennett?"

He shakes his head. "I haven't seen him yet. We've been busy getting the offices ready for the new councilmembers. Is he a councilman if he hasn't taken the oath yet?"

"Good question. They've elected him," I say, searching my brain for state law. "Members of the legislature, and all public officers and employees, are required to take an oath of office in California. I would think the oath-taking is legally part of it because it's required. I'll have to ask one of the city attorneys. "You might ask at the Legal department. If you do, come back and tell me the answer."

"I will," he says and beams like I've given him a mission.

I realize I'm standing on the chair with a short skirt on and he's dreamily staring at my legs. Samir's not an adolescent—he just graduated from San Jose State—but he has that look teenage boys get when they have a crush. It's a pretty safe bet that he's still a virgin.

"Is there anything I can help you with?"

He glances up to my face. "If you're hanging up pictures, I can do it. I can find a hammer instead of you using your shoe."

Samir is sweet, but I'm not in the mood to entertain him today. I'd rather do this alone, even if I'm using my unpractical high heel.

If nothing else, it will keep my mind off of Jax. "I'm just hanging a calendar. Thanks for the offer to help, but I'm almost done."

He glances around the office for another task he might do for me. He's done this before, but there's nothing he can suggest to prolong his visit.

"If you change your mind, just let me know," he says and heads for the door.

"Thanks, I will."

I turn back to my project. I'm able to remove enough pictures to make a space for the calendar. I'd hang it on a nail that's already protruding from the wall, but it's in the wrong spot. I pull it out to reposition it when there's light tapping on my door again.

"Ms. Ivarsson?"

I turn to face the door, waiting for another excuse why Samir should help me. "Come in."

The door swings open, revealing a shiny new Jaxson Bennett in a dark custom suit. "Chloe?"

Surprise pitches me forward. I grip the tall bookcase to stop myself from falling off the chair.

An alarmed Jax rushes in. "Whoa, be careful." His hands are moving toward my waist, but he stops short when he realizes what's about to happen.

I steady myself before I topple over and hold out my hand that I'm alright. He's close enough to catch me, if I take a tumble. I breathe, glad the danger has passed, but we're staring at each other wondering what comes next.

"You don't want to break your neck and then I'd have no analyst to work with," he says and flashes a watchful smile. "I'm sorry I surprised you." He chucks his chin at the door. "I did knock."

I'm beyond uncomfortable meeting him again without warning. My hand grips the bookcase tighter. I still might fall, if I let go too soon.

Jax steps back, giving me space to adjust. He's older, and if it's possible, sexier than his photos. The pictures of him before the campaign had him with a morning-after sex stubble along his jaw. The man standing here looks the part of a rising political star with his thick blond hair short on the sides and a clean-shaven face that displays his dimpled cheeks where the angels kissed him.

"Hi. Did you come to the city early to check out your office?" My delivery is still unsteady, but what does he expect when he scared the shit out of me?

He leans against the desk and gives me the official councilmember face, reserved for constituents. "Guilty. I wanted to see my office, but I also wanted to see my Chief of Staff, which they told me is you. I couldn't believe it when they told me we're working together."

Standing on the chair, I'm beyond uncomfortable trying to reconcile that we're here talking.

He offers his hand. "It looks like you're trying to hang something on the wall. I can help you with that."

I take his palm and the old feelings come rushing back like a shot of adrenaline. I step off the chair, settling close to him, staring into the face of my old love.

The shift from high school to college was difficult my first quarter. My roommate got mono that fall and had to leave school a few weeks after we started. They'd been promising a replacement, but it'd been nearly a month with no new roomie. I didn't miss her; we were never friends, and she spent most of her time in her boyfriend's dorm across campus.

Jax and I had been dating for a few weeks since a chance meeting during a break between classes in the student union when he asked to sit at my table. At the moment we met, all homesickness vanished.

We spent most nights in deep discussions and went out after midnight like two night owls prowling the streets to open all-hours art movie theaters, coffee shops, and dive restaurants. We'd talk about everything from art to politics, but the subject always came back to legacy and what he'd contribute to his family's story.

Councilman Bennett is observing me with an odd expression I can't read. Something is going on behind those intense hazel eyes. Could he be remembering our past, or were we having a shared vision? He moves forward, his hand on the shelf above me, face looking down at me. My body tingles, breathing in his faint aftershave and the familiar scent of him underneath that expensive fragrance. I can't believe he smells the same after years apart, like he marked me with it to make me know it's him.

Tapping at the door interrupts the moment that still seems to linger. The intensity of our attraction surprises me, like we're back in my dorm room. I continue to hold his attention, willing the visitor to give up, but the knocking is more insistent. I close my eyes briefly. I don't care if it's the mayor, I'm going to take the head off of whoever comes through that door. I take a step away from Jax. "Come in," I say, not hiding my irritation.

Samir pokes his head in again. His wide eyes and gape betray his surprise at finding Jax standing next to me.

"Sorry if I've interrupted. Hello Councilman-Elect Bennett," he says with an embarrassed stutter.

Jax gives him a nod.

"This is Samir, an intern working in the council offices."

He nods back, then aims his attention to me. "I found this hammer and I thought you might need it. I'll leave it here on the desk."

No shoes and standing too close to Jaxson Bennett will be all around the city in two minutes.

"Thanks, Samir, I appreciate it."

"No problem." He backs out and shuts the door.

Jax pulls on the cuff of his shirt. The monogrammed cufflinks are visible for a moment. The mood has shifted to cordial business with a colleague. It wouldn't be right to rekindle a relationship in this

21

tiny office, although it might be memorable.

"I think that intern has a crush on you."

I wave a dismissive hand toward the door. "Nah, he just likes to help."

Jax snags the hammer from the desk and holds out his hand to me. "If you'll give me a nail and let me know where to place it, I'll hammer it in for you."

I drop it in his palm and we move to the wall. He's staring at me, slipping back somewhere in his mind. Could we pick up where we left off or is it just me who's feeling a moment in our past and wants it back?

"You can put it right here." I press my finger to the spot.

He places his hand next to mine, then brushes me briefly to place his finger in the exact place. I move behind him to give him space to work. The office seems smaller with Jax's big body. We'll have to work in his councilman's office if we want to get any work done. A couple of taps and the nail is in the wall. He cleans powdery residue away from where he created the new hole.

"You know Maintenance will have your hide if they knew you're driving nails into the wall," he says.

A nervous giggle escapes. "Lucky for me, I'm friends with the head of Maintenance. He's been turning a blind eye for years. He's also said that if I ever leave, I'll be spending my last day filling in each of these nail holes."

Jax lets out rumble of laughter and shakes his head. "An analyst who's well connected. I like that. Now what would you like me to hang on this wall?"

I want to ask him about the past, but it can wait. I never dreamed that this would go easily.

I hand him the calendar. He strips the cellophane off and tosses it in the trash. His back is turned to me as he fumbles for the right month. He stretches toward the nail to hang it up and adjusts it a bit, then stands back. I peer around him to see his handiwork.

The firefighter I spoke to this morning is on the current month. He's standing in the kitchen with food and lots of kitchen gadgets, preparing a holiday meal. It can't be in the fire station; it looks like a trendy home or a set. He's wearing a blue-striped chef's apron, the kind that attaches at the neck and waist. He's tying the apron about his waist, looking straight into the camera with that same bad-boy grin I saw earlier.

The photo is meant to showcase him entertaining in his kitchen in a typical "at home for the holidays" theme, but he's got nothing on underneath the apron. The front part is flopped down, exposing his massive chest but not revealing his interesting bits. It looks like the first scene of a bad porno movie, just before they play that cheesy sex music.

I don't get it. The calendar cover was an architectural drawing of a building; he didn't mention it would be fire cooks pin-ups. Embarrassment burns my cheeks that Jax thinks I'm a desperate, horny woman.

Jax crosses his arms, appraising the calendar like it's a fine art piece. His dimples are out, supporting a smirk.

"You have interesting taste in calendar art, Ivarsson. I had you pegged as a lover of architecture, landscapes, or cute kittens. I see you have a wild side."

I'm saved from responding when an alarm goes off. He glances at his watch and stops the chime.

"I'm sorry to cut this short. It's later than I thought. You can tell me all about it later. I've got guests coming for the swearing-in. You'll be there?"

I nod.

"Great, we can talk after. I know you have a lot of questions."

23

Family Business

*I*n a rare sweep, all eight incumbents up for reelection lost their seats out of a fifteen-member council. This has rocked city government, at least for the councilmembers up in the next election. But today is not the day to analyze why. The press will gleefully provide, for each candidate, in detail, which opportunities you failed to use to your advantage or how brilliant and nuanced your political acumen. So today you will either be joyous or philosophical about your fate, depending on the outcome of your race.

The swearing-in is a private session with the mayor and in the next regular council meeting, the new members will take their oaths again for the public. The gallery is packed with friends and family ready to share in their success as each member takes a long-awaited victory lap before the hard work begins, trying to keep their seat for another term.

I close the door to my office, then pat the pocket of my skirt again to assure myself I've got my phone and keys. These functions can be long, so it's best to travel with only essentials. I maneuver my way across a crowded quad of visitors dressed in their Sunday best, heading to the council chambers.

Dominica and I snagged seats in the back row of the gallery. I like this advantage; I can see everyone on the council floor and crowd reactions to the ceremony. We sit back to endure speeches and congratulations for the new officeholders until all eight councilmembers stand to take the oath administered by Judge Madrigal.

I watch Jax's solemn face as he repeats his vow, ready to serve his country, state, and district. It wasn't so many years ago I saw my future in that face. Jax coming back into my life has got to mean something. The question is, will it lead to a happily ever after?

The vice mayor does the closing remarks and invites everyone for catered refreshments. During this time, Jax will mingle with his guests and take pictures with the mayor, colleagues, and family. All the incoming councilmembers will have an official portrait taken as a group today, then individually for the lobby of City Hall at another time.

Dominica pulls on my arm. "Do you see all those women crowding around Jaxson Bennett? I think part of your job is going to be fending off the female population."

Jax's rich-guy good looks made him popular with women, but these young eager females crowding around him look like fans. I'm guessing they might've worked on his campaign to be invited to this private session. One female appears to be asking a question, and Jax looks like an intent listener until his chin tilts, his gaze searching the crowd. He finds me among all these people and gives me a ghost of a grin. I smile back, warmed by his attention that starts my stomach fluttering. It's not fair that after all this time, I still want him as much as I did when we were teenagers. I'm worried about our meeting later, when we'll have time to talk. He returns his gaze back to the woman still talking. I don't think she even noticed he wasn't listening to her.

Dominica leaves my side in search of Cheryl. She can't leave the councilwoman too long on her own or she'll send someone to find her. I stroll closer to the dais. I'm deciding whether to approach Jax to congratulate him now, or wait until we have our meeting later.

"Jaxson told me I'd find you near the back of the room, but the way he described you..."

I turn.

The man scans the room. "He said to look for a dark-haired beauty with big brown eyes and a captivating smile. Are you Chloe?"

I nod at this stranger.

The man extends a meaty hand. He's about fifty and has thick, dark hair with tadpole streaks of gray, and he's portly like a friendly Santa Claus. "My name is Mitchell, by the way."

I take his offered hand and shake. "Do I know you?"

"No, but you do now. I'm Jaxson's campaign manager." He throws a worried glance at Jax, who's still in conversation. "Don't tell Jaxson about the beautiful comment. I don't want to get him in trouble."

"Don't worry, no one will hear it from me," I assure him.

He nods, shoving his hands in his pockets. "So, what do you think of our boy pulling off a big political coup? We were certain that we weren't going to win in the last days of the race...that's why we held the victory party at a low-rent hotel downtown."

"Yes, a huge surprise," I say. It was enough of a surprise for me to lose my wine and cocktail appetizers down the toilet the night he won. "Councilman Bennett is savvy enough to make an excellent politician."

He rocks on his heels, speaking with more seriousness. "Of course, this is a stepping stone to bigger things. If he has a successful run on the City Council, there's no telling where he could end up. Believe me, he's the full package."

Jax is mega-rich in his own right, but he tries extra hard to give off the vibe as just another guy. Both sides of his family have old money, and with his personality, he was never in danger of being ordinary.

I'm thinking of a polite way to leave. I'm not in the mood to hear his political plans for Jax after his term is over. I'm a policy nerd and all I'm concerned with is legislation that will help this city.

He stops speaking and studies me for a moment. "I apologize. I didn't come by just to talk your ear off, although I'm capable of doing that. Jaxson sent me over. He was afraid that you'd leave before he introduced you to his family."

I blink at the notion. Of course his family would be here. I scan the crowd again. Off to the side of his female fans is an older woman with three males.

Mitchell glances around to see who's near us, but I'm still focused on his family. He lowers his voice. "You're looking in the right direction. That's his family over there. The striking redhead is his mother, Jessica Bennett, his father, Stephen, and Jaxson's two older brothers, Fletcher and Larson.

This means something if he wants me to meet his family. I turn away from the scene; eventually they'd see me staring at them. That wouldn't be a great first impression.

"If he's going to introduce you to his family, I thought it best to prepare you."

I'm impressed. With all his blustering, he's a good campaign manager. Never let the client go into the lion's den without intel.

"Jessica is a grande dame, and used to getting her way, so I advise you to tread softly around her and agree as much as possible. You can speak up and you should; she can't stand mousy women."

I nod, taking this in, like I'm in a required life class.

"You don't have to worry about Stephen. She's the dominant one in the family and whatever she likes, Stephen likes. Her husband is interested in things like cars and painting. As far as I can tell, Jaxson isn't one of his interests, but the mother and son have a strong connection."

I don't have a problem relating to men. I'll have to research his father, which is easy enough. I'll need to find some common ground if it isn't his son.

Mitchell pauses like he's searching his brain for more information. His eyes narrow when he hits on the right data. "The two older brothers were teenagers when Jaxson was born, so they never were very close. One's a doctor and the other one is a lawyer, but I can't remember which one. Jaxson has always looked up to them. He's the youngest and wants to be taken seriously."

I glance back at Jax. So, he's the baby. If it's a strong bond, I'll need to undo some of the mother's influence to make him spouse material.

Mitchell tries to catch my gaze. I slide my attention back. Later is for making plans. "You need to know that making money is expected in that family, but political power is their legacy. Jessica's father was a State Senator, from somewhere back East, and his mother wants Jaxson to go beyond what his grandfather accomplished. That's them in a nutshell. You have a lot of experience handling different constituents, so I'm sure you'll be fine..." His gaze travels to the council floor. "Hold on." Mitchell is acknowledging something across the room. "I see the opening I've been waiting for. Follow me."

I'm aware of each tempered step I take as we draw closer to the group of Bennetts. They haven't noticed my approach yet. I feel like a prisoner on Death Row, with someone about to yell out, *"Dead woman walking."*

Jax gives me a reassuring smile that it'll be alright. All I can manage is to show my teeth in a weak response. We weren't together long enough to talk about meeting family. I knew he was close to his mother. This has to be a huge deal if he starts off wanting me to meet her.

Jax makes his apologies and breaks away from the crowd to take the last few steps with me and Mitchell toward his family. I know

Jessica from the social column. She's a household name in her circle. I'm bolstered on either side by Jax and Mitchell. If my knees buckle during this introduction, I'm sure they'll catch me.

"Mother, I'd like you to meet Chloe Ivarsson. She'll be my policy and legislative analyst; she's also my Chief of Staff." I extend my hand and the woman clasps it warmly.

"It's nice to meet you, Chloe. Mitchell has told me wonderful things about you. It appears you're the reason Peterson was successful getting through his legislation. I hope you'll do the same for my son."

"Thank you for the kind words. I'll work hard to support Councilman Bennett's agenda." What else was I going to say under her heavy scrutiny? Analysts are impartial government employees, not elected officials. We support the City Council no matter the administration or political affiliation.

Jessica lightly touches the arm of the distracted man that looks like an older, shorter, sour version of Jax. "This is my husband, Stephen, and these are Jaxson's older brothers, Fletcher and Larson." Each man extends his hand and I shake them in turn. I'd say the only person who wants to be at the ceremony is Jessica. The two brothers are a lot like their father in mannerisms, with Jessica's auburn hair. They're pleasant enough, but they're not present. Jax is like an excited puppy and beams at his family. It's a shame his enthusiasm isn't infectious; it doesn't appear to be shared by his family, who treats his accomplishment as something expected.

Jessica gently pushes in between me and Mitchell. Slipping her hand under my arm, she urges me to take a few steps away from the circle.

"I don't know if you're aware, but I come from a political family and I was the one who convinced Jaxson to stop wasting his time as a CEO and try something more meaningful." Her attention drifts to Jax talking to his brothers, and she maneuvers me further away from their hearing. "My father started his political career on the City Council, and he never regretted that experience. It helped him to launch his Senate career." She brings her gaze back to me to make her point. "It's important for my son to have savvy people around him who are fierce supporters. Between the two of us, I believe this will be the first step in a very impressive career. I hope you don't mind, but I'll also be helping Jaxson. It's good for a politician to have several perspectives."

She plans to be a shadow adviser, an influence outside of his staff. This is a big city. Jax will have a full team to work with. I'm the senior analyst and will help lead the team. I need to articulate our goals a little clearer. "Our first team meetings will concentrate on his agenda for the first year, what he can focus on to make a quick impact. We'll also outline goals for his entire term, identifying the major issues he wants to tackle, but remaining open for other opportunities that affect his district."

Her eyebrows raise as I rattle off more jargon, but I got the reaction I wanted.

"Mitchell was right; you know your job." She clenches my arm tighter, like a restraint. I almost wince at the pain. "Let's makes some time to talk," she purrs like we're best friends.

"Mother." Jax comes up beside me. "Please don't scare Ivarsson. I need her to get me through my term. It's her job to guide me through this new world."

I'm grateful that he's attempted a rescue. He's looking at me with an unfocused gaze and I think he's going to take my hand to reassure me it's alright.

Jessica clears her throat and my attention jerks back to her. She's watching me, curiosity narrowing her eyes. She glances at her son, who hasn't responded. Suddenly, she doesn't seem as friendly.

"If I can have your attention for a few moments." The vice mayor is tapping the microphone. A blare of sound peels through the air in protest, enough for me to cover my ears. "Sorry, everyone, but the photographer is ready if you would like to take pictures with the mayor and your families. He's set up in the side anteroom."

"Stephen," Jessica calls. He comes to her side, followed by her sons.

Jax watches the guests making their way to the temporary photo studio, then back to me. "Are you coming?"

"These are official photographs; only family is appropriate," Jessica huffs.

"She's right," I say. "This isn't time for staff photos."

He studies the stream of people heading to the anteroom. "Could you all wait for me in line?" he says to his family. "I need to talk to Ivarsson for a minute."

Jessica looks at me while addressing her son. "Don't be too long…we don't want our turn to come and you're not there."

"I won't," he assures her. "Please, you know you don't want us to be the last to take our pictures with the mayor."

Her husband offers his arm to a skeptical Jessica before another objection, and they stroll away with their sons trailing.

"Will you wait?" Jax says. "It shouldn't take long."

"I shouldn't intrude any longer on your day—"

"I want you to wait," he says, cutting me off.

I remember this look, jaw set, eyes intent; there's something on his mind.

"Okay," I relent, "I'll be here."

The gallery is filled with people who didn't make the cut to have a picture taken with a councilmember. I turn to trudge up the center aisle. I'm searching for a seat when I hear, "Hey, Chloe."

There's a man in the first row grinning like he knows me. I figure he's a friend of one of the councilmembers or someone I met at one of the endless events I attend for work. I should wear my glasses, then I could really see his face from this far away. I give him a tentative wave and he motions for me to come near. We're in a crowded room and he looks harmless enough…what trouble could I get into just talking with him? As long as he's not press, I'm fine. I hike to the end of the row and stop.

"Hi," I say.

I'm near enough to see his disappointed face.

"You don't remember me?

He's handsome and looks familiar, but I can't place him. "I apologize that I don't remember your name; did we meet at an event?"

"It was kind of an event for me. I met you this morning on the street. My name's Brody."

Right, I remember now. He's the hot firefighter that charmed me out of all my cash. The uniform must be a big part of what I saw this morning, and that's why sex isn't rolling off of him in waves at the moment. I must have a firefighter's fantasy tucked deep in my psyche. His pair of jeans and a navy T-shirt with a firefighters' emblem where a pocket would be has dimmed his sex aura. All I feel is a strong pull toward him, which isn't unpleasant.

"I think I would've remembered you straight away if you came in in your firefighter's gear."

"That guy you were talking to with his family…" He glances toward the dais. "Is he a boyfriend or a husband?"

That's kind of presumptuous. He's known me all of not even a day and is asking personal questions? "No, that's Councilman Jaxson Bennett. I work for him."

He tilts his head, thinking. "It didn't look like that from here and I could hear your conversation. You work for him? What do you do?"

I walk into the row and sit down beside him. "I'm a legislative analyst."

"What's that, some kind of secretary?"

Who calls support staff secretaries? "No, I'm not support staff or an admin. I help write legislation, represent him at community meetings, things like that."

"I thought you were an admin."

I can't tell if he's teasing. "Well, I'm not." Since we're both being honest. "This is a closed event. How were you able to get in?"

He shrugs. "I found out where you worked, but when I got to your office, they said you were here. I know the security guard at the door and he let me in."

"I owe you money," I blurt out, remembering why he's here.

"Yeah, and I'm here to collect."

"I don't have any money on me. But I have the donation at my desk. I don't know how long I'm going to be here. Can you pick it up tomorrow, or I can take it to you?"

He shakes his head. "I'm working tomorrow. I'm on a two-day rotation, so this is the only time I'll have."

He thinks I'm going to stiff him for the money. "I could drop it by Station 38?"

He relaxes back, manspreading like he has all the time in the world. "I can wait till you're done." He chucks his chin to the dais. "Your boss is coming back."

5

How You Remind Me

*J*ax strides onto the council chamber floor alone, looking like he's already a fixture in city government. He pauses, his tall form and blond head easily identified among groups of visitors; he's searching the gallery. As if I hear his silent call to me, I'm pulled up like a marionette toward the center aisle without a goodbye to Brody. Relief lightens Jax's face when he sees me dodging people to get to him.

"I promised it wouldn't take too long," he says when I reach him.

I'm happy the niggling doubts that he'd left without telling me were wrong.

He throws a glance back at the line for photos. "My family will be here soon. Mother is giving pointers to the mayor, telling her how to run the city. I have to give it to Monica…she's indulging her, and they're talking like old friends."

He doesn't offer more insight, so we fall into an awkward silence among a sea of guests. You'd think we'd have an endless supply of stories from our lives to share from a dozen or so years we've missed.

His gaze lights on a new councilmember, who's shepherding his skipping daughter through the throng toward the anteroom. They nod to one another.

"I didn't have time to say this earlier, but I want to congratulate you on winning your council seat."

The green flecks in his eyes appear to darken as he searches my face. "I didn't think you'd be that welcoming to me for winning my seat. I thought we'd have an adjustment period where I'd have to convince you not to resent me for taking your old boss' place."

It's a fair assumption, but it still strikes me as funny. I have to remember he's new and doesn't know how all of this works. "I'm a city employee," I try to reassure him. "I'll be here through many councils and administrations. My goal is to help you get stuff done."

The faint smile on his face says I've amused him. Maybe the traffic patterns today were wrong, and I'll have a good day.

"Good to know. Mitchell didn't go over that part during my briefing. I've had to play catch-up since this unexpected win, but I'm a quick learner."

Mitchell and Jax's family join us and the atmosphere turns artic with an icy wind blowing toward me.

"Talking strategy already?" Jessica asks, her gaze settling briefly on me. Her face softens when she steps close to Jax to smooth down her son's lapel. "Jaxson, you'll have more than enough time tomorrow to make plans. I think you should concentrate on celebrating your win and cementing your relationships with your donors and key constituents."

He ruffles at her attempt to control. "What mother is saying," Jax says without turning away from her, "is that she has arranged a party to do just that."

"A party?" Mitchell turns on an unapologetic Jessica. "This is the first time I'm hearing about it. I've asked you several times, Mrs. Bennett, to be an assistant or co-campaign manager. I value your support, but I should be informed when you arrange these soirées."

"Mitchell, you always call me Mrs. Bennett when you're cross with me. It's only a small party and not worth mentioning. There are people I want you to meet."

Mitchell looks interested for a few moments, then shakes his head. "All right, I give up. Please promise to let me know in advance from now on."

"I will, Mitchell." She touches his arm, which doesn't reassure him her promise will be kept. "Now that that's settled," Jessica says, hardly hiding her victory, "I suggest we go soon. I've reserved Manresa for the evening."

I take a step away from the claustrophobic circle of Jax, Jessica, and Mitchell. Her husband and sons stand a few steps away, engaged in their own discussion, but close enough to hear our conversation. "I hope you all have a lovely and productive evening." I direct this to the three of them, reserving a second goodbye to her husband and sons. "It was nice meeting all of you," I say.

Jax's concern falls on me. "I know you're hearing this last minute too, but you're coming, right?

Jessica intervenes before I can respond. "Jaxson, you know Chloe is not political; that isn't her function. The attendees will be party members, donors, and supporters. Besides, I know she'd be bored… it's a working party."

A muscle ripples along his jawline, and it's the only tell that something is brewing under his polished surface. "Chloe is my senior policy analyst. It's important for her to know what's on their minds. I'll need her advice."

I ignore Jessica's disapproval and touch his arm to stop the escalation between them, because a big part of my job is to stay ahead of potential problems. "You can brief me tomorrow, before our staff meeting. You'll be fine. Mitchell and your mother are here to help; just don't commit to anything until we talk." I say this to Jax while looking at Jessica. His mother gives me a half smile that doesn't reach her eyes. Another minor victory for her.

"Jaxson," Jessica appeases, "even Chloe understands. There will be other parties and strategy sessions."

I nod at Jax, willing him not to take this further. He ignores me. "This has nothing to do with meeting donors. She's declining because you haven't made her welcome."

Her eyes narrow, like she's trying to read the fine print on a document. "As I've pointed out, this is a working party. Is there something you're not telling me?" She looks at me. "Have you met before?"

I glance at Jax. What's he going to tell her, that we met in school?

Mitchell has been observing this scene without comment. This standoff has even caught the attention of the rest of Jax's family.

"So, this is a personal relationship you haven't told me about?" Jessica accuses.

"Yes, I admit we've met before." He gives an exaggerated glance at his watch. "Two hours ago, when I went to her office to meet her."

I free myself from Jax and step away. Standing in the middle of the crowded council floor isn't the place to discuss details about our relationship, but he could at least admit we've met before today.

"I understand this is a working party." Jax says the words slowly to a frowning Jessica. "It would be helpful if Chloe met these supporters. She understands the district and can discuss issues more confidently than me stumbling my way through something I know little about."

"The two of you seem very familiar." She glares at me for answers. "I'm sorry if this is uncomfortable, Chloe. I don't like deception, and I need to understand what's going on."

I have nothing to say. The explanation, whatever it is, should come from Jax.

Jax squares his shoulders, a protective hand still on my arm as he addresses his mother. Our small group is an uncomfortable collective witness. Jessica shifts, capturing her necklace, but continues to expect an answer.

"What I know about Chloe and the rest of my staff comes from my meetings with Mitchell. I stopped by her office before the ceremony. I was concerned there'd be some animosity because I replaced her boss. When I met Chloe for the first time, she wasn't what I expected. I was surprised we hit it off. Mother, this is a professional relationship, nothing else."

I met Chloe for the first time - This is a professional relationship, nothing else. It echoes like a shout down a canyon. "It's true, Jessica," Mitchell chimes in.

I angle my gaze away from Jax, to Mitchell, who's happy to be the center of attention.

"What Jaxson knows about Chloe comes from my background check." His apologetic gaze lands on me. "There was nothing personal in the material I gathered, only information you'd find in a resume or public documents. We wanted to know how effective you and the rest of the staff were at your jobs. You shouldn't worry…it was all positive."

Jax's palm lands lightly on my shoulder, and my instinct is to brush it away. Right now, I'm more curious to know what the hell is going on.

"I'm sorry about the investigation," he says, "but it's standard stuff to know who you're working with. I'm looking forward to us working together."

He doesn't fucking know me. All this time, he's been treating me like one of his political groupies. I clamp down my emotions to make sure they don't show. "Thank you for inviting me," I say to Jax, "but the people at the party want to talk to you. I know you can convey their concerns to me. We can talk about policy and legislation tomorrow. This is a celebration and you should be with your family."

Jessica's pitying smile signals she's happy that I've accepted her wishes, and that she has squashed any imaginary romance between her son and me.

"I'll be in the office tomorrow at 9:00, Councilman Bennett. We can meet to discuss the party in the morning." I acknowledge Jessica and her family standing behind her, waiting to go. "It was nice meeting you all."

I blindly stomp across the quad towards my office.

"Hey, Chloe."

I keep moving. I don't care who's calling me.

"Hey, Chloe, wait up."

I whirl around, ready to lash out to make this pain go away. "What?!"

Brody catches up with me, his hands in the air. "Don't bite my head off. I'm not the guy that acted like a jerk."

I'd forgotten Brody was in the front row. He heard and saw everything. Not only am I angry, but I'm embarrassed this stranger is a witness. "You want your money, is that it?"

"I want you to take a breath and calm down. I know he's your boss, but did he mean something to you?"

"No…yes, why do you want to know?"

"I just want to help you; you're upset."

I don't speak, I just stand there looking into his concerned face. Why would this man care what happens to me?

"Look, you need to vent, so why don't I take you to a place where I go to let off some steam? I go there when I'm pissed at the world." He points to the parking lot. "See that black two-ton truck over there? That's mine. I'll take you there and we can talk."

"What about the money I owe you?"

"Fuck the money. Excuse my language, but you're more important."

I'm eyeing him while I consider his suggestion. This big, brawny guy looks like he belongs in a superhero's suit, but isn't that what a serial killer posing as a firefighter would do to lure an unsuspecting woman to her demise? "Sorry, I don't know you." I side step him and start toward my office.

He's gotten in front of me again, walking backwards with his hands up like he's trying to get me to slow down. "You can talk to the security guard at the door; he'll vouch for me."

I halt and stare at him. "You're asking me to take the word of someone I've never seen before?"

He rakes frustrated fingers through his dark hair. "Okay, I see your point; that's not a great idea." He turns to his truck. "Why don't you take a picture of me, my truck, and the license plates and text it to someone you trust? You can continue taking pictures of me as long as we're together."

His ideas are getting more ridiculous. I'm ready to turn him down again, when the sound of voices and laugher capture my attention. Groups of people are spilling out of the council chamber. Small clusters of people are heading toward the public parking lot on the north side. Jax appears, and he's a bright light strolling among the crowd with his family. He's laughing as his mother places her hand on his shoulder. I think I can hear his laughter from this distance, but it's only in my memories. Blood squeezes from my heart as I watch him disappear from view.

I turn to Brody. "Let's go," I say as I push past him. I'm almost at the truck when he realizes I've accepted his offer. He jogs to catch up. When he overtakes me, he pulls a key fob out of his back pocket and the door locks pop open. I slide into the cab and pull the seatbelt across my lap. I pull out my phone. He places the key in the ignition and I snap a picture of his profile. "Please look straight at me." I snap another photo of his surprised face; he shakes his head.

"Why the fuck did I suggest this?" he mumbles.

I tap out a text to Kellis as the truck kicks to life. "What's your last name?"

"Knox. I can give you my driver's license and Social Security number if you need it."

"That'll be great. I'll collect it later."

6

Brute Force

We say nothing while he maneuvers his truck through the city. I'm not registering the landscape, just brooding about Jax. My muscles are tight with anger from his Judas denial of him not knowing me.

I saw it, felt it. There was no denying a spark of attraction that flared between us in my office. If Samir hadn't interrupted, we might have kissed; it might have been the beginning of him remembering me.

Honking brings me back to the truck moving through traffic. We're on the north side of the city in a sprawling industrial section. What could be here among garages and sheet metal works?

He pulls up in front of the grungiest building on the block. Grime or maybe black paint covers the windows. It looks like an old warehouse. The brickwork was probably stunning back about a hundred years ago. The hastily painted sign above the front door says: Brute Force.

I pause on the sidewalk while Brody saunters up to the entrance. He holds the door open, looking back at me. "I promised I'd take you to a place you could let off steam."

I slip my phone out of my pocket and snap a picture, then hit send before pushing it back into my pocket. I squint up at the sign. "I thought you were taking me for a drink. Is this a bar?"

He shakes his head. "You don't need a drink; you need to hit something." He pushes through the door and, before it swings closed, I'm through the entrance. I've never been in a boxing gym before. At least, that's what I think this is. The dead giveaway is there's a boxing ring in the middle of the space. The place looks like a throwback to gyms in black and white movies from the forties. A large, graffitied wall is the one update.

Among the tags on the wall are portraits of boxers, some of whom I recognize, like Mohammad Ali and Anthony Joshua. A few people are scattered around the large space, working out. There's the clank of metal at the weights rack, punching of leather bags, general sounds of exertion, and pungent old sweat.

"Where have you been keeping yourself, handsome?" a sultry voice drifts from behind us. "It's been a few weeks since you visited me."

Brody turns to give a lopsided grin to a tall, athletic woman in a tank top and jeans. Tattoos swirl about her well-defined right arm. You rarely see a woman that beautiful with no makeup. God, this must be his girlfriend.

"Don't be like that, Lindy, you know I always come back to you."

She leans against the doorjamb of an office, brushing back a wisp of auburn hair that escaped her French braid, giving Brody a no-shit expression. "Are you bringing your dates here now because you've run out of places to take them, even though there's a perfectly good Applebee's down the road? Or are you trying to make me jealous?"

He transfers that grin to me. "Chloe, this is Lindy. She and her

44

father, Frank, run this place. And when she's not running the gym, she's giving me grief."

"I'm only giving you what you deserve." She smiles sweetly. "What are you doing here? Is Chloe going to watch you box?"

"I thought I'd teach her how to punch the bag."

A 'ha' escapes her. "No offense, Miss Chloe, but I've never seen anyone in here with four-inch heels and a suit looking like she just escaped from a business meeting."

Brody takes me in for the first time.

I shrug, my frown siding with Lindy. "You should've told me we were going to a gym."

"Now hold on," Lindy interrupts. "I don't want you to get a bad impression of Brute Force. You can still hit the bag if that's what you want. I have some stuff in the back you can wear if you don't mind that it's not designer."

I almost start laughing, but she's serious. I glance around, sizing up the place, trying to look like I hang out in boxing gyms all the time. "It's fine with me; where do I change?"

When I return, Brody has already warmed up with a jump rope. He places it on a bench and reaches for a water. A light sheen of sweat is showing on his chest and broad shoulders, exposed from his black muscle shirt. His cut-off sweats hit just below the knee. This gym must be a regular hang-out for him. I flash back to the pin-up calendar where he exposed more of his body, and I get lost in that image for a few moments.

I'm uncomfortable in this new workout wear. I resist the urge to pull at my tight tank top that has Brute Force printed across my chest. I also have longish shorts that say Brute Force down one leg. Lindy even had sneakers. I bought this outfit from the equipment section of her office. Good thing I always have a credit card tucked in my phone cover.

I tie my hair back into a ponytail, waiting for my lesson to begin, then fish my camera out of my pocket and take another shot. I don't need another photo, but when am I going to get a candid picture of Mr. January from a firehouse cooks calendar in his workout gear?

He places the bottle down and looks me over critically. "You're a lot shorter without your heels."

"Thanks for pointing that out. I thought we were gonna slap around a bag?"

"You'll punch the bag. Did Lindy give you any practice gloves?"

I pulled the pair out of my pocket. The gloves also say Brute Force. I slide the gloves on, worried that my manicure might not survive this training session. "Did you know she has an activewear boutique back there in her office? Their logo is on every piece of clothing."

"I know. I bought a couple of hoodies from here. Have you ever jumped rope before?"

"The last time I jumped rope, I was probably eight."

"Stuff like that you never forget." He hands me the rope.

I grab it and start a slow hop, jump, hop, jump to the one potato, two potato rhyme in my head, not able to capture the old jumping rhythm.

He folds his arms, evaluating my performance. "You jump like a wounded cow." He sticks out his hand and I slap the rope back into his open palm. "Let me demonstrate." He holds my gaze and jumps like it's his job, with two feet, then only one, in a quick rhythm, letting me know he's nauseatingly fit. He stops and hands it back.

"Come up on your toes one to two inches off the ground. Elbows in slightly." His hands touch my arm to adjust me. I lift my gaze to his face and he's turned up his sex aura. The same feelings are back from our first meeting and I'm tingling. His warm palms slide down to my hands.

"Everything happens in the wrists," he says.

How can I sustain anger when he's looking at me like that?

He stops the brief demonstration, slipping back into coach

mode. "Try it again. Jump twice, stop and jump twice again, stop. Continue until you have it down."

I take a breath, avoid his judgmental gaze, and try. It takes a few times, but I'm able to jump rope a few seconds before tangling the cord. It's hard work, but I keep trying until my heart is pumping and I break out in a sweat. He smiles. "Good job. I think you're ready to punch."

I leave the rope on the bench and bounce on my toes like a fighter loosening up. It's more to calm jitters for being out of place here or maybe being with him.

He laughs at my antics. "I like funny women," he muses. "Come on, Sugar Ray, we're going over here."

We move to an area where five long bags are suspended in a row. A guy who is almost as big as the bag is doing rapid-fire punishment to the one at the end. Sweat pours from him while he dances and weaves with precision as the over-stuffed leather pouch lumbers back and forth. I'm amazed at the display of skill; I've only seen boxing in movies or on TV.

After giving the bag a last punch, he turns to us, raises his gloves to gesture a goodbye, and walks deeper into the gym.

Brody motions me in front of a bag while his other arm cradles it like he's getting his arm around a bear. "Go on, take a shot."

I square my shoulders and dance a bit.

"Come on, hit it, you're not at the prom."

I step up about half an arm's length to the bag. I pull my right hand back and slam my fist into the tough leather. "Ouch," I say, jerking my fist back. I shake it to relieve some of the pain in my wrist.

"I didn't know you were so pissed," he says with a chuckle. "You have a good right for girl, but you need to know how to punch. If you keep hitting like that, you're going to break your wrist."

He releases the bag, then shows me how my fist should land. Then he pulls his other hand to his face, steps forward, and strikes

47

the bag. "Leave your fist a bit loose and strike at this angle. Get in the habit of keeping your fist up and close. When you jab, make sure the other hand is up protecting your face. Try another punch." He grabs my hands to pull them up in place.

I do what I'm instructed, aware that his eyes are on me, evaluating. I strike the bag.

"Good," he says, "you have potential. That can turn into a skill if you practice. Let's try a series of punches. Let's do a combination of two–four–two. Two rapid punches followed by four slower, then two more."

He demonstrates. We practice the two–four–two combination slowly, then do it more rapidly, until I seem to have gotten into a rhythm.

"So has your boss always been a jerk?"

I stop the combination and hit the bag with one hard punch. The impact makes him take a step back. "He hasn't even been my boss for an entire day." I take another shot.

"Looks like you and your new boss got off on the wrong foot."

"He and I have met before, a long time ago."

"Was he a jerk then?"

"Technically, we met in high school. But he never noticed me. He was one of those hotshot kids on the water polo team and his girlfriend Portia was the bouncy blonde head cheerleader."

"I get this now; you don't like cheerleaders?"

"Nope, because I was a cheerleader bouncing right alongside her. Every time we cheered at a game, I'd look up into the stands and he'd be staring at Portia. Well, everyone stared at Portia because she was one of those blonde Nordic beauties."

I abandon my punching to answer Brody's questions. He's making me relive the past, and even now I can feel how anxious I was for Jax to see me.

"When did he notice you?"

"We were going to Santa Clara University. I'd spent time near the business department hoping to see him, but that never happened. I was having lunch in the student union when he came by my table and asked if he could sit in the seat across from me."

"So why didn't you live that happily ever after shit?"

I let out a sigh. "I thought we were. We dated for a few weeks. They were the best weeks of my life. I know people say that, but I can remember every day with him."

"Then what happened?"

"Princeton happened. Although I don't know for sure. All I know is that we spent one amazing night together. I thought there would be more, but he left without saying goodbye."

"Your boss is acting like a jerk because you knew each other in the past and he doesn't want to own up to what he did?"

"He doesn't know me, Brody. He doesn't remember me or the night we spent together."

"Are you sure?"

"I thought he knew who I was when he came to my office before the swearing-in. We had those same sparks like we did years ago. It was a brief encounter, but he asked me to come to the swearing-in. Later, he sent his campaign manager to find me so I could meet his family."

I turn away from Brody because this is painful to admit. "I guess the vibes I was getting from Jax were what he throws out to all his female staff. He says the only thing he knew about me was from the research his campaign manager provided. They wanted to know how effective the staff and I were at our jobs."

"That sucks."

"Yeah, it sucks to be me. I'm stuck working for a man who doesn't remember me or how much I care for him."

"Then hit the bag," Brody urges. "Imagine it's the fucker's face and you're smashing it in. Hell, I'll teach you how to do a roundhouse kick and you can aim it at his balls."

I look at him with my mouth open. Is he serious?

"Hit the bag, Chloe." He pushes the mass slightly towards me. I jump back and hit it on the backswing. I punch. It feels good to challenge my muscles and get some of this contained anger out. Brody stops the swinging bag and holds it for me as I continue to jab at the anonymous piece of leather in front of me. I jab and forget that Brody is standing near me. I keep jabbing so I won't have to feel pain, don't have to think about what it will be like tomorrow when I have to walk into his office and act like nothing's happened. I keep jabbing and all this time Brody holds onto the bag, watches me, and says nothing.

Even five minutes is a long time when you're not used to that level of exertion, but Brody encourages me to keep pushing myself. If he said anything after that, I didn't hear him.

I strike, draw back, strike again like a rapid-fire machine only aware of me, the bag, and the pain I'm fighting through until the sweat runs down my face and my tank top sticks to me. It goes on forever, like I've been in this trance for hours. I'm dulled enough from the exertion that I could push on longer. But it's my body that protests. My contact with the bag slides off with no impact, ending the session.

The effects of my punches vibrate through my arm as my gloved hands fall loose at my sides. I'm wobbly, panting, and less angry.

Brody releases the bag. "Looks like you needed that session. You want to keep hitting?"

"No, I think I should change and go home."

He points his thumb over his shoulder somewhere past the ring. "The female lockers are that way. When you finish changing, I'll meet you in the office."

Great, he's going to talk to his girlfriend.

I shower and stuff my workout clothes in a Brute Force shopping bag. When I get to the office, Brody is leaning against the doorjamb talking to Lindy, who's sitting at her desk. They both turn to me when

I approach.

"Ready?"

I just nod. "It was nice meeting you, Lindy, and thank you for helping me pick out all the gear."

Brody moves away from the door to stand next to me. Lindy walks out of her office. "You're welcome, Chloe. I hope you got a good lesson. If you're interested, there's a women's boxing class on Wednesdays. If you don't mind getting hit, come join us."

She says this with a challenge in her eyes. I like Lindy. I'm sure Brody told her I wasn't his date. I hope she's not suggesting the class as revenge. I study her and dismiss the thought. Her face seems too open for her to be devious.

"I'll think about it."

"No pressure, it's an ongoing class. We have women with all skill levels attending. We find that the more experienced women help the newbies and they're a great bunch of females. I think you'd fit right in."

Brody parks his big truck next to my car.

"Thanks for the boxing lesson," I say as I unfasten my seatbelt. I push the door handle, ready to slide out.

"You're welcome, anytime. If you want another lesson, let me know."

It might be fun learning to box. I push the door open.

"You know, if you want that guy back, you're gonna have to do something about it."

I turn back. He's looking at something in the parking lot, not bothering to meet my gaze. "What can I do, plan an intervention?"

"He needs to see you as more than someone who can advance

his career."

"How do I do that?"

"It shouldn't be hard; you did it before." He looks at me. "You need to make him jealous."

I pull the heavy door closed and twist back into my seat. "How can I make Jaxson Bennett jealous? The man can have any female; why would he want a lowly analyst?"

"That guy doesn't care about what you do for a living. It's who you are. Look, guys are only interested when they see other guys going after the same prize. You create some competition, you'll get his interest."

"You're suggesting I make myself into a trophy?"

"That's what I'm saying. Find someone to be the other competitor. Some guy who doesn't have skin in the game that will help you out. That way, you can work as a team and get an unbiased opinion while you're making the guy jealous."

Thinking of myself as a prize to get a man was a new concept. "Are all men like this?"

He shakes his head and gives me an *Are you serious?* look.

"It won't work. I don't know anyone like that."

"Why not? You're good-looking enough."

"Gee, thanks for the compliment. Anyway, thank you. I liked the lesson, and I enjoyed meeting your girlfriend."

Brody's eyebrows shoot up. "My girlfriend?"

"You know, Lindy. You must be a great boyfriend. I bet you don't even remember her birthday."

He rears back to let out unrestrained laughter. "Me and Lindy ain't gonna happen," he says between his stupid guffaws. "Her birthday is October 13th."

"Why not? Do you have a problem with gorgeous women?"

"Believe me, I wouldn't mind tapping that. If Lindy is interested in anyone, it would be you."

I look at him like he's grown another head, which at this point wouldn't surprise me.

"Lindy likes women. Unfortunately, she's not bi. You know, come to think of it, she has a girlfriend. If you're interested, you've got bad timing. She's off the market, anyway."

He's trying to restrain another round of laughter. "That was a joke," he says.

I pull out my phone and snap a photo.

"I guess you needed one more for the road," he says, not hiding his grin.

"Thank you, Brody. I appreciate the lesson. You're right, punching a bag was better than a drink."

1

Sexy German Men

"Schatz," Kurt bellows without looking up from his laptop. "The wandering Chloe has finally returned." He's at the kitchen counter, still in his work clothes, a blue cotton shirt with neatly cuffed sleeves enough to reveal his wolf tattoo on his left forearm and dark jeans. I still can't get over the fact that the work attire in tech companies is that casual.

Kellis bustles into the room, pulling a towel from her wet, bobbed hair. She looks settled in for the evening in blue Lululemon sweats until she catches sight of me.

"Where have you been? Why didn't you answer my texts? Why were you sending me pictures of a hot guy?" She says this all in one uninterrupted breath.

Kurt's head shoots up from his work, interested in his wife's questions. "Chloe, are you sending dick pics to my wife?"

"Hello to you, Mr. Heinrich," I scowl. "Why would I send—that doesn't make sense—never mind. No, I didn't send Kellis dick pics."

He gives me a teasing smirk, happy he's got me rattled, then returns to study his computer. "Then what were you doing that you had to send pictures to Schatz?"

I yank open the fridge, ignoring their questions and concentrate on a kitchen that lacks the signs of dinner prep, unless it's frozen food night, that no one told be about. "I thought one of you roomies would have started dinner by now."

Kellis kisses her husband on the top of his close-cropped hair, then slides into the chair next to him. "Kurt has already ordered from Naschmarkt, that Austrian restaurant in Campbell. He knows the owners. They're sending us some dishes Kurt's been craving that are not on the menu."

"Proper food," Kurt half mumbles. He throws an admiring look at Kellis. "Good food for my Schatz, that will help the baby grow."

She meets his gaze with the same devotion. I love them both, but sometimes I feel left out when they begin their knowing sidelong glances.

I clear my throat so they'll remember I'm here.

"Chloe," Kellis says, forcing her attention back to me. "Why don't you change? The delivery should be here soon, then you can tell us what's going on with Jaxson over dinner."

I lean against the fridge, surprised she outed me to Kurt. It's not a secret, just awkward he knows I'm struggling with Jax back in my life. This doesn't help my clear-eyed older sister reputation.

"Don't look at me like that," Kellis says. "I had to tell Kurt about Jaxson Bennett. He's just as concerned about your happiness as I am. Look at this as a good thing. Kurt can give us a male perspective."

Kurt finds his wife's hand and entwines their fingers. "I want to help too." His teasing is gone. "You were in my corner when I tried to get this stubborn one to fall in love with me. Let me return the support you gave us."

Kurt and I were friends when they were enemies, and we're still friends. I go over and kiss my brother-in-law's bristly blond head too. He beams at me and I trail off to my bedroom.

"Call me as soon as the food arrives. I'm starving."

"All that happened in one day?" Kellis says, stabbing at her plate.

"I guess I had an eventful day. I was hopeful in the beginning, then it all when to shit quick."

Kurt absorbs our conversation in silence. Once I finish my story and Kellis is still chewing, he sighs and folds his arms to signal an end to his no-comment policy. "Do you want my opinion?"

He's dead serious. I nod, curious to find out what he thinks.

"I think you working for Jaxson would be difficult no matter how you view the situation. The tension between the two of you will affect your work performance. You don't want this to tarnish your reputation; never risk that. There are two options to consider: asked to be transferred to another city councilmember or give your resignation."

"Hold on, husband. She has another option."

Kurt frowns, not used to someone contradicting him. This must be what it's like to be the king or CEO of a huge corporation. "I reviewed every plausible alternative. If there's another choice, I fail to see it."

She spears a micro potato and points it at him. "Brody suggested she plan a seduction." The tiny item lands safely in her mouth and she continues her thoughtful chewing.

Kurt shakes his head. "That's too risky and it could backfire."

I'm running through their suggestions in my head when I realize I haven't mentioned the Assistant Manager position. That job could be another problem. If I ask to be assigned to another councilmember, then I'd need to let Jax know why I don't want to work with him.

If I resign and leave the city, I'd have no chance at the position. I'd lose my insider's edge.

Kurt is right about making Jax jealous—it's risky and I'm not the person to pull off a big deception.

"What Kurt says makes sense, but I still need to think about it."

"Just for the sake of argument," Kellis speaks up. "Why don't we examine Brody's suggestion? I think it's the least risky option. And if you can find the right man to help you, your job won't be in jeopardy."

"That means I have to turn into a sexy witch to lure him back into my bed." I imagine my tailored wardrobe; I'm not equipped to seduce anyone wearing a Brooks Brothers suit.

Kellis breaks into my thoughts. "You're in this for the long haul, right? I mean we're talking about a long-term relationship, marriage?"

"I want to spend my life with Jax."

"Then we need to find the right man who's willing to help. He's got to be good-looking," Kellis says, ticking off an imaginary point. "Successful would help, although that doesn't need to be part of the criteria."

"I don't know anyone like that," I say, trying to stop this now, before Kellis attaches to this impossible idea. "All the men I know are government workers, and he'd hardly be jealous of one of them."

"Right, then we need to look in our own backyard." Kellis taps her finger to her lips until her eyes spark. "I think Matt Westmore would be perfect, but then again, he doesn't like drama, but he might make an exception."

"Matt's a jerk," Kurt grumbles. "He'd probably screw it up."

She waves away his suggestion. "You'd say that because the two of you don't get along."

That was a diplomatic way of explaining the two men's intense dislike for one another. Kellis was dating Matt when Kurt decided to blow up their relationship so he could have a chance with my sister.

It's Kellis who's preserved Kurt and Matt's civil working relationship at Drachen Technology.

"This is true," Kurt concedes. "I will say that he's good at his job. He's a strong leader, but he's still a jerk."

They turn to me for an opinion. I've only met Matt a few times. He's one of those high-powered CEOs.

"I don't know if I could be convincing with him. He seems a little intimidating."

Kurt throws up his hands. "That's because he's a jerk."

Kellis lifts her eyes to heaven, shaking her head. "Don't listen to him; Matt's a really good guy. He might do it if I ask. But if you're not comfortable, then let's think of another possibility." She considers for a few seconds. "How about Riku, he's an HR analyst at Drachen? He's cute, but he's younger than we are. If you think you can pull off the older woman/younger man, I know he'd do it."

"I remember him," I say. "Lots of charisma. Looks like a K Pop star. I think he'd be perfect, if he was a bit older."

I knew all of Kellis' friends before she met Kurt. If she suggests ex-boyfriends, we might be here all night.

Kurt's rubbing his chin like he's working out his suggestion. "If you insist on finding a man, there are some young men in our management team at the Munich office who I think might be a match for you. I can have their pictures and resumes sent to you tomorrow. If you like any of them, I can have them flown out to meet you."

Kurt's off-handed suggestion is enough for Kellis and I to stare at him. HR in Germany must be flexible if they can ask employees to do him a favor. But then again, he's the head of a multinational company. I'm sure he can make it happen, but I'd feel awkward interviewing men to be my fake boyfriend.

"Thank you for the offer—that's very sweet of you—but I'd rather find someone I know."

"You know, no one is sexier than a German man." He says this as if it's a quantified fact. "Ana, my admin, is an excellent judge of character. She'll select pictures and resumes today. I'll ask her to email them to you."

"Love," says Kellis to her husband, "why would Chloe need to see their resumes?"

"To know how exceptional they are," he says, as if this is obvious. "I can vouch for all of them. I hired each man for my executive team. I want my sister-in-law to know she's selecting from the best."

I don't want to offend Kurt. His intentions are good, even though he's overprotective with the people he cares about.

"Sure," I agree, to let him think I'm on board with the idea. "I'll take a look at the German studs."

"You won't regret it," he says, pleased with my decision. "I'll email Ana now; she needs to begin her research."

Chloe stacks our plates and brings them to the sink. "Thanks for including him. You know he only wants to help."

I remove the rest of our glasses and utensils from the counter and join her at the sink. "I know. That's why I agreed to him pimping me to his team."

Kellis rinses the dishes and stacks them in the dishwasher. "It's not like that—well, maybe it is. No matter, we'll deal with that later. Tell me what you've decided to do about your new boss."

"Tomorrow Jax meets the rest of his staff and he's scheduled to meet some of the other councilmembers for a one-on-one. That will give me a buffer for a large part of the day. If it's too uncomfortable during my alone time with him, I'll do what you suggest and exercise my options."

Kellis reaches for a towel and dries her hands while studying me. "I don't envy you right now. Jaxson has stumbled into your work environment and upended your life with just his appearance. Decision time might not come tomorrow." She places the damp towel on a hook. "You could have a few days or even weeks to decide. Whatever you do, you might not realize the effects until much later. This is big, important stuff, so take your time."

There's no solution where I come out a winner; it will be, at best, a compromise. If I stay, I'm forced to make peace with a man that I've never forgotten and continue to live with the pain I carry from our break-up. I realize break-up is not the right word; that feels like it implies an agreement. It's closer to abandonment. How do you get over someone you love when he leaves you behind without a goodbye or an explanation?

Kellis checks the kitchen one last time for anything we failed to throw away or place in the dishwasher. "No judgment," she says. "Kurt and I are here for you, and we'll help in any way we can; just let us know what you need."

I feel better with support and options and, although the *let's make Jax jealous* plan is outlandish, it's better to go to battle with something.

Kellis switches on the dishwasher. "You better remember to text me tomorrow, and I mean with hourly updates."

8

Fruit Bowl

I arrive at City Hall earlier than normal and head for Arlene's office. She's the head of HR and I've known her for a long time. She's a great person to bounce concerns off of and keeps my confidences. I want to give her a heads-up that there might be problems. It's better to begin this conversation now, before I'm forced to make a change.

It's my bad luck when I reach her door and peer in through the glass panel; she's not there. I think about grabbing a bagel, but instead I go to my office. When I open the door, there's an enormous fruit basket obscuring most of my desk. I hunt for a card, but there's nothing. This is something Kellis would do. Come to think of it, her style is more chocolate and champagne, and she'd leave a note, something encouraging.

I drop my purse in the bottom drawer of my desk and ease off my heels. I tap the voicemail button and listen to my messages. Most of these calls will pertain to Peterson, my old boss. I'll have to do some callbacks and let them know that he's no longer the councilmember for District 5.

Between scratching a caller's name and number on my pad, my gaze wanders to Brody's face regarding me from the calendar on the wall. I hum a tuneless melody, remembering yesterday with him. That boxing lesson would have been fun if I wasn't in a state over Jax. I doodle a brawny Brody Knox in a black muscle shirt on my pad, instead of taking the information from a caller that's leaving a long message. She finally hangs up. There's silence before the next message begins.

"Ivarsson, are you there?"

I stare at the desk phone.

"This is Jaxson." He clears his throat like he needs time to find the words. Then his confident voice booms again. "I hope you got my fruit basket, and if you didn't, you're getting a fruit basket."

I glance back at the fruit explosion on my desk.

"I want to apologize for my mother. She means well, but she can be a little aggressive when it comes to my life. As I suspected, that get-together was not a working party. There was a lot of socializing and congratulations for winning my seat. I'll be in at 10:00. I want to talk to you before I meet the rest of the staff at 10:30. I'll drop by your office."

10 o'clock comes and Jax hasn't appeared. I'd arranged for the rest of the staff to meet us in the small conference room at 10:30 a.m. I figure something happened to him and he was in an accident that must've involved his hands. Because that's the only reason he would have to prevent him from texting me if he's delayed.

"This guy is already twenty minutes late. In college, if a professor doesn't show up for class after fifteen minutes, we can leave," says Mateo, a junior analyst who has a lot to learn about being patient.

"He should be here any minute," I say to everyone in the conference room.

Patricia shrugs, staring down at her cell. "I don't care if he makes me wait all day; I get paid for sitting here playing games or working. It's up to him." The other two staff members, Miley and Vargas, are munching on the donuts I brought as a welcome to Jax.

He's already forty minutes late and still no explanation. I decide to let them all go back to their cubes. "I'm sorry, everybody. Something must have happened to Councilman Bennett. I'll send out a new notice when I schedule the next meeting. In the meantime, make sure your reports are ready about your current activities and be prepared to talk about any upcoming issues that the Councilman should be aware of. Thank you for your time."

Chairs scrape against the floor as the staff gets to their feet. I walk to the donut box, planning to leave it in our kitchen area.

"Aw, hello Councilman Bennett," says Patricia, slipping her cell into her pocket and backing up while Jax is entering.

"How's everyone doing?" Jax flashes a smile around the room. "Sorry I'm late. Some last-minute things came up." He sits at the head of the conference table while we find our seats. "I've been looking forward to meeting all of you." The staff returns tentative head bobs to him and WTF pleas to me.

I stand behind Jax to mouth a *calm down* to the staff and take my place to Jax's right. "We've been eager to meet you as well, Councilman Bennett," I say and make the staff introductions. The newer members are nervous, attempting to make a good impression. I've already prepared them to discuss their roles, their areas of expertise, and what they're currently working on. Before we hear their reports, Jax interrupts.

"As you know, this is my first time working for government. I'm eager to work for the benefit of our district and the city. I'll be relying on your knowledge to guide me. Since I was late today, I missed my meeting with Ivarsson. I would like to conduct that meeting now with her, and after, we will send out another meeting date. Thank you all

65

for coming."

Twenty minutes after sitting down, the meeting is over with nothing accomplished. The staff trails out of the room and I'm left alone sitting with Jax. I watch him, not knowing what to expect. He leans back in his chair, his lips forming a thin, resigned apology. "Looks like I managed to screw up my first staff meeting. I figure if we talk now, we can make this right for the next meeting."

"How can I help?"

He gives a deep sigh. "First, you can tell me what the hell I'm supposed to do."

"I don't follow; about what?"

Jax rubs the back of his neck. This is a tell he still has when he's uncomfortable. He stops when he catches my gaze. "I'm from the business world. It's pretty straightforward; we sell a product for profit. Here I know I'm supposed to be improving people's lives, but I don't know how to go about it."

Peterson was already a councilmember when I became a legislative analyst on his team. He had years in the job and his staff was a well-oiled machine. With everything else I worried about, teaching a new councilmember the ropes wasn't first on my list.

I pull out my laptop and open up my docs program to a new page. "Okay, let's start with the basics. Each member of your team has a specific role to play and we work within our swim lanes. For example, Mateo does transportation, public works, planning land-use, and energy. He's well-versed in these sectors, and you can rely on him if questions or concerns come up within those areas. My expertise is public safety, public health, fire, and police. I'm not only an analyst, I'm also your Chief of Staff. I'll be working with you more closely than the rest of your team. My role is to guide and advise."

"I'll be honest, I thought the Chief of Staff title might be more administrative. I'm glad you're here to help pilot this ship. I'd have a tough time without you." He lets go of enough tension for the corner of his mouth to quirk up. "What do we do first?"

"I suggest easing into the position. Let the team continue working on policies and issues they've already started. What we need to figure out is in what direction you want to take this district. I've arranged a tour this week. Schools, hospitals, some key small businesses. You also have a few large companies in your jurisdiction. You might know their CEOs already."

"I know them and I don't anticipate a problem with that group; they all supported my campaign."

"Great, then what issues do you want to tackle?"

"You're my policy wonk, what do you suggest?"

I type the word issues at the top of the page and place a number one under the heading. "Many councilmembers run because there's an issue they are passionate about. What platform did you run on?"

"Bringing government into the 21st century. Better access to services and giving districts a bigger say in what happens in their own backyard."

"It sounds like a lot of vague promises, with nothing concrete, but that's good...it means there's a lot to choose from. Peterson worked a lot with the mayor on access to food. During his time, he created more food pantries and free food buses that went into at-risk communities."

"I agree we should continue the work—it's important—but I don't want to follow the same path of my predecessor. We need something big that will not only impact the district but the city."

I stare at the blank page, then back at him. The past and the present fighting for attention. I stay in the now and consider his request.

He moves onto his elbows, pinning me with sharp hazel eyes. "Ivarsson, I know you can do this. Find me a big enough cause that will have television cameras in here when we announce our plans. You and I can start a new era and make everyone take notice. With you by my side, I know we can do this."

Jax is a natural persuader; they voted him most likely to charm the birds out of the trees in high school. Those years on the debate teams in high school and college have served him well. Does he want to help people, or are we pretending to care to heighten his public profile? He's already famous in the Valley, so no matter what he does, everyone will notice.

"Ivarsson?"

I blink to bring him into focus. He was still talking while I was in my head.

Annoyance is etching small lines in his forehead. "Did I lose you for a minute?"

"I was working through possible issues. It will take some time to find the right cause. Then there's messaging to consider—"

"I know it's a lot to take in. Why don't you take the rest of the day off and think about how we can move forward? Let's have a breakfast meeting tomorrow and you can pitch me your best ideas. I'll text you the time and place." He pushes away from the chair and strides for the door.

I've just glimpsed my future with Councilman Bennett. This is an abrupt change from Peterson's inclusive style of how to best serve the district. Jax holds the door open.

I scramble to my feet, scoop the laptop off the table, and meet him at the door.

"I know I sound demanding on the first day, but I'm used to driving the process until we have results. This is a chance to make our mark. It might be a good idea to work the team like a business; I think it will make us more focused as a group. I know there might be some pushback, but in the end it'll be worth it. Let me know if you need anything from me."

I'm left watching him advance confidently down the corridor. We went from staring at each other with doe eyes in my office the first day to him ordering me around like his girl Friday in some black and white film. The absolute worst thing about this shit show is that he's using my last name, like I'm one of the boys on his team.

Arlene's office is at the north end of the building. I pass through the rotunda, side-stepping tour groups as I go. I need to speak with her now. I promised Kellis I would see how my first day went with Jax before I made my decision. I tap on her door.

"Come," she says as I push the door open. "Chloe, nice to see you. Are you excited about working with Councilman Bennett?"

I shut the door and slide into the seat in front of her desk. "The short answer is no."

Caution widens Arlene's eyes for a few moments until her features morph into something noncommittal. "I met him during the swearing-in ceremony, and he seemed like a lovely man. Has something changed?"

I've got to get this out before I think about it rationally and back down. "I'd like to be placed on another councilmember's staff. I hear Councilmember Marquez is looking for a policy analyst."

Arlene doesn't hide her confusion. I know she wants to ask me a million questions. "Yes, Marquez is looking for an analyst, but they want to bring in a junior. You're too experienced for that position. Tell me why you want to make a move…has something happened?"

"I don't think we're compatible."

"Maybe I can talk to him on your behalf. He's new and doesn't know how government works."

I shake my head. "No, we're way past that."

She's wringing her hands. It's dawned on her I'm serious and she can't talk me down. "I see…and when would you want to make this change?"

"As soon as possible. That brings up another concern. I hear that the Assistant City Manager position will open soon."

Shock wipes the neutral expression off her round face. At that moment, I remember that Dominica told me that HR didn't know about the resignation. "I mean, I heard a rumor, and I was just wondering if it was true?"

Arlene takes in a breath. "Yes, well, we can't believe every wild rumor we hear. I'm glad you came to me to ask about that. No, the Assistant City Manager is not resigning. At least, I haven't heard anything."

"If the rumor ever becomes true, I'd like to be considered for the position. I have the qualifications and even have the experience with the city."

"If it ever comes to that, I'll let you know. You know we always like to hire from within, and I think you'd be a candidate they'd consider. I'd put in a good word for you with the search committee."

Arlene thinks the Assistant Manager leaving is unlikely, or she'd never have thrown out an offer of support. She's too savvy an administrator.

"Thanks for the endorsement. That will be helpful if the time comes."

She sits back in her chair, more confident that she has some control over the situation. "Now, the matter of working with another councilmember, as far as I know there are no other openings in any of the districts. But as soon as I hear of one, I'll let you know. In the meantime, I would suggest giving it a little more time with Councilman Bennett. He's probably nervous about his new role. I think that you're the best person to guide him through the maze of city government."

I can't flat-out quit to get off the team. It's not about the money; I can always work for my mom if it came to that. I want that job in the City Manager's office, and I'm too close to my goal to have Jax or anyone else stop me.

"Why don't you give it a week?" Arlene says, slipping into her HR manager counseling role. "You can come back here to discuss how you're feeling. If you're still determined to make a change, we can explore other possibilities at City Hall. Can you do that?"

At least she knows I want to move…that's something. I don't

want to be perceived as difficult. "Yes, I'll give it a week and I'll come back here and we can talk."

"Sounds like a plan to me."

I might as well begin my day off now. I glance at my phone. I've got time to run an overdue errand before I head home.

9

Falling Ground

There are more cars in the visitor's parking lot than usual, so the only space open is a hike away from the entrance. I've been here before with Councilman Peterson, but never by myself. The building is a low brown structure from the '80s. It's had several upgrades over the years, but it's like plugging holes in a sinking boat. Fire stations have changed with new equipment and technology that makes it a tight fit for the guys that work here. It would make sense to level this station and build a new one in its place.

The uneven parking lot is a freaken obstacle course, and it has me maneuvering in these heels. Even if they don't have funds to build a new station, they should find money somewhere to repair the lot. I'll call a contact in transportation to ask when this parking lot is scheduled for repairs.

A female, all business in her blue uniform, greets me at the desk. "Welcome to Fire Station 38. How can I help you?"

She looks familiar until I realize she's the female firefighter who was holding the calendars the day I donated to their cause.

"Is Brody Knox working today?"

"Do you have an appointment with him?" She just became more business, if that's possible.

"I bought a calendar on Monday when you were out on Tanner Road. I didn't have the money then, but I promised to pay him later. I came by to give him my donation. He told me he'd be working today."

She picks up a phone. "There's somebody to see Brody; is he back there? Yeah, I'll tell her." She places the phone down. "He's still in a meeting and I don't know how long it will take."

I don't have to see Brody to give him the money. It's not right to wait for another time. "Do you have an envelope? I'll slip the cash inside and you can hand it to him."

She rummages in a drawer, finds an envelope, and hands it to me. I stuff the $30 inside, seal the envelope, and pick up a pen from her desk. I write: *This is my donation for the calendar. Chloe Ivarsson.* I give her the envelope.

I'm doing a balancing act on the badly pot-marked pavement of the lot. Maybe it's my vanity that's kept me in these heels instead of changing into the sensible shoes I keep in my car. A tiny pebble rolls under my feet, and that quickly my heel catches a divot in the cement. I spill forward, landing hard on my hands and knees. I'm a bit dazed down on all fours, swearing that it's the last time I wear four-inch heels in this damn parking lot. I gingerly push to my feet, careful not to re-injure myself. The scrapes sting like hell, but I'm more annoyed about the fact I fell than the pain in my right hand and knee. At least the lot is empty.

"Hey, are you all right?" Brody shouts.

"Shit."

He's doing a jog toward me, his face pinched with concern. "I saw the fall from the station. They haven't paved this place in a long time. The city is lucky we don't break our necks out here."

I brush dirt from my skirt with my good hand while holding the other away from my body. I frown at the picture window that takes up most of this side of the building. He might not have been the only one that witnessed my tumble. "I'm fine," I say, pissed. "It was just a little spill. All women know that if you wear high heels, there's a possibility you might fall off of them," I say, trying to joke it off. I guess he didn't get the humor because he's concentrating on my hand.

"Do you mind if I look at it?"

I stick out my hand. He cradles it in his two big, warm palms. He's gentle as he turns it over to see the back.

"The scrape is just on my palm and my knee," I say to get the inspection over quickly.

"You're bleeding," he says, giving me his diagnosis. "The scrape isn't deep, but you need to clean it now. We have a medical kit inside for the team. I can dress it up for you."

This is the second time he's come to my rescue. He'll be offended if I don't accept his help again.

"Come on, I'll give you a Tylenol for the pain and I'll even throw in a tour of the station…deal?" It's his soothing encouragement that has me saying yes.

The worn examining table sits in a tiny room at the back of the station. Brody washes and dries his hands. He reaches for a small blue box and pulls out a pair of gloves and a medical kit from the top shelf. He rolls over on a small gray stool that gives easy access to my knees.

"I'm going to clean the wounds. I'll start with the gash on your hand," he says, making sure I understand.

I got a tiny shiver off that reassurance. It's hard to ignore my reactions when they're unexpected. Better to concentrate on the prickling pain and less on him. I extend my hand.

He tears open an antiseptic towelette, unwrapping it carefully. "This might sting a little," he says, and he applies it to my hand.

I try not to be a baby, but I squirm anyway, and he holds my palm tighter.

"I know it hurts." His voice is rumbling low. "But I'm almost done." He tosses the pink-stained towelette into a trash, finds a tube of antiseptic cream, and applies it to the wound. "You're being a very brave girl," he says, applying a Band-Aid to my hand. "Now let's check out that knee."

He's just tending to my wounds, but it seems sexier when his rough fingers brush the perimeter of the scrape. It has me holding my breath and glancing up at the ceiling until his gentle touch forces me to watch as he cleans the wound and finishes with antiseptic and another Band-Aid. It's the contrast of how a big, powerful man can be so caring. He smooths the plaster over my knee. "We're done here. I think you'll live."

"Thank you, Dr. Knox. I think you missed your calling; you should've gone into the medical profession."

Instead of the expected chuckle I thought I'd get, he shows no emotion and turns away as he pulls off his gloves.

"I'll keep that in mind, Ms. Ivarsson." He goes to a cabinet and retrieves a bottle of Tylenol, opens the top, and shakes out two into my waiting palm. He produces a bottle of water from a small refrigerator. I take the pills with a water chaser.

"Are you ready for the tour?"

"In a minute," I say, still curious. "The fire district is in need of EMTs and paramedics. Are you interested in the program?"

"I am, but the department doesn't provide that training for free and I don't have the money. Are you ready to see the station now?" he says, ending more of my questions. I didn't want to tell him I'd already been on a tour of the station several times and always with the chief.

The tour was a casual behind-the-scenes working of a fire station, instead of the stiff, polished tours I'm used to. I enjoyed it more because it was with a nice guy who actually works here with his team. Before I thank him and say goodbye, he invites me to sit outside where the team goes to relax.

We take a seat on a bench looking out at tables, chairs, and a basketball court beyond that.

"Thanks for the donation. If I knew it was you waiting for me at the desk, I would've come out sooner."

"How's the donation drive going?"

He stretches his long legs out in front of him. "That's the meeting I was in. We were going over the figures."

"And?"

"And we've been at this for almost a year and we're nowhere near our goal."

"Will you continue your fundraising efforts?"

He shrugs. "We have to...there's been a rumor that were' re not getting the additional funds we need."

"What have you done as fundraising activities?"

He shoves his hands in his pockets and looks at the court. "Direct solicitation of the community, like a pancake breakfast or crab feeds, is the only thing we can think of to bring some money in."

Station 38 is in District 5. I brought this issue up to Councilman Peterson, but he didn't feel any motivation to help or even push for funds. "I think you're going to need a bigger fundraising effort."

"The pancake breakfasts and our crab feeds bring in a lot of money."

The wooden bench creaks when I shift my weight to cross my legs. That bandage on my knee doesn't look appealing. "Community outreach is fine, but you need to reach out to companies," I say.

"We've made appeals to the local companies. Some have given

us donations, but they've been small."

"You have to give companies more bang for their buck, like a fun run?"

A frustrated frown looks back at me. This is important to him. "The fire department has enough money to underwrite pancake breakfasts and crab feeds; what you're talking about is going to take a lot more money."

"Hey, Brody, I thought you were going to show me how to make bolognaise?

The blond rookie I saw on Monday is standing in front of us.

"Tyler, this is Chloe."

He gives me a grin. "Hi, I didn't see you there. Brody promised to teach me how to cook."

"I'll be there in a few minutes, after I walk Chloe out."

Tyler gives us a stiff salute and heads back inside.

Brody walks close to me, monitoring his patient as we travel back to my car. "How's life with your boss?"

I lean against the car, looking up at him. "Difficult. I've asked for a transfer to another councilmember's staff, but I have to tough it out for a week before they'll do something."

"Maybe you can avoid him for a week?"

"That would be ideal, but no. I have a breakfast meeting with him tomorrow, or I will when he texts me the time and place."

He moves in a bit and I can feel that sex aura again—the intense gaze, his mouth perpetually turned down a little at the corner like he's seen it all...probably he has. I'm still trying to figure out his appeal and why he has it without trying.

"You decided not to make him jealous?"

I flatten my back against the car. I'm getting flashes of me bent backwards on the hood with his big, hard body weighing me down and his mouth on mine. I take what I hope is an unobtrusive step out of aura range.

"I've decided to cut ties as soon as possible, and I want a chance at the Assistant City Manager's position."

I regret telling that bit of information. No one knows about that opening and no one knows I'm interested, except Dominica and Arlene.

"You have higher ambitions?" That seems to surprise him.

"Even in school I wanted to be the City Manager of San Pacitas. It's not something a little girl usually dreams of doing..."

He doesn't comment, just shifts his weight to lean his arm next to me. I'm caught up again in his presence, and this time I don't want to step away. We're searching each other's face for a sign, waiting or hoping for the other to make a move. His face is a vivid portrait with the smooth, strong jawline, blue eyes made more intense with this onyx hair that appears to resist his efforts to tame. A few stray locks rest carelessly on his forehead. He shifts again, and it looks like he might kiss me, and I think I want him to try.

"Brody," Tyler screams from the entryway, his hands cupped near his mouth to increase his volume. "They're calling a meeting. The captain sent me to find you."

Brody looks back at the building.

I slip a little further away from him, realizing how this might look to everyone staring out of the office picture window.

"Shit, I'd better go," he says, his attention back on me. "It was good seeing you. If it gets to be too much with your boss, call me and I'll meet you at Brute Force for another punching lesson."

10

Breakfast Club

I get a text from Jax just before bed. I'm to meet him at his house in the hills for an 8:00 a.m. breakfast.

I'm traveling up a narrow winding road, the path more suitable for an Italian sports car than my Japanese sedan. I chug up to the top of the hill, turning off into an open gate. The property road expands out into a wide driveway. I park the car in one of the spaces, pull the emergency brake, and just stare at the spectacular view of the valley cloaked in light silver-blue mist. Now I know why that winding road is worth the trouble.

Much of the house is made of glass. The architect was going for an outdoor feel in this heavily wooded area. A pool that glistens from here extends out to the edge of the property. A low, solid wall faces the lot. I pull out my lipstick and apply a thick coat of deep pink to calm my unease.

After my meeting with Jaxson Bennett, I decided I wouldn't work for the Silicon Valley CEO who's accustomed to his every whim being carried out. I might have weathered that, or even helped him to adopt a different style for government, if he had remembered me. Reminding him now would introduce awkwardness, or worse, him lying about a false recollection to pacify my hurt ego.

The cool, crisp breeze lifts my hair away from my shoulders while the balls of my feet crunch the crushed stone path. I push the doorbell and hear chimes echoing throughout the house. There's a rustle in a nearby bush. I take a cautious step away from the shrubbery. I hope that's a bird; nothing should slither around here in the almost-country.

A plump woman with a ruddy face that looks like she's been working all morning stands in the doorway. "Miss Chloe?" she says, arching a thick blond eyebrow.

"Yes," I smile back, not knowing how to address this woman.

"I'm Brita. Come."

I step inside the foyer. There's a hallway to the right, but a screen separates the foyer from the main house. The scent of baking with notes of cinnamon and apples drifts from the long hallway.

She wipes a hand on the side of her flour-dusted apron that covers her broad hips, then sticks her palm toward me. I shake, feeling the strength in her grip.

"I cook." She chucks her chin toward the hall, like I should know the location of the kitchen. "Mr. Jaxson's assistant isn't here. You can find him and your breakfast out on the terrace." She gives me a frank up and down. "If you don't like the food, I can do something special." She turns away, lumbering her way down the hall. It seems pointless to say thank you to her back.

Stepping around the screen, I can see the terrace, but the space I have to traverse seems endless. It's an open, modern home with little furnishings; beautiful, but stark. Jax is leaning against the railing, back to me, taking in the view of the valley when I arrive at the deck. There's a strong urge to run to him and wrap my arms around his neck, so he can lift me up for a kiss, like he's done many times before.

82

"Councilman Bennett?" I call out.

Jax doesn't turn to face me, as if he's taking a few moments to come to the end of his contemplation.

"Ivarsson," he says with slight annoyance. He turns, the view at his back. A crisp gray dress shirt and slacks set off his hazel eyes that appear mildly disapproving. "When we're alone, I'd like you to call me Jaxson, or Jax, if you like that better." He says this in a way that draws you in.

He's a charmer, he works hard at his *I'm just a regular guy* persona.

I glance at the view like I'm considering his suggestion. "Okay, Jax it is," I say, smiling, because when we met, I called him Jaxson, until that changed.

He introduces himself as Jaxson. I never heard anyone shorten his name. It's a few days after we begin dating that he becomes Jax.

When you're young, you want everything in your life to have meaning. We were no different. We saw everything that happened to us as destiny and saw confirmation in the smallest of occurrences.

It's one of those nights in the middle of October, the kind where the cold of autumn hasn't arrived, and it gives you the false hope that summer will continue all year.

That night we're restless and, on impulse, we drive to a concert at Shoreline Amphitheatre. I don't remember the name of the band, but I remember we were desperate to see them. When we arrive at the box office, the only tickets available are lawn seating.

We haul a blanket and a sack of food up to the top of a grassy slope away from everyone. We don't care that we aren't down in the front rows to see the band. The giant screens on either side of the stage are enough for us; it's the music we want to hear. I sit in front of Jaxson, me leaning back into his arms, his long legs on either side of me. Nothing, since that night, has been more perfect.

We sing, kiss, and laugh through the concert. We even dance at the end until the last note of the encore dies and the lights switch on, erasing the magical night world.

Jaxson slings the food bag and our stuff over his shoulder, and we file out into a mass of people moving toward the exit. Jaxson is behind me, his hand at my back. I'm claustrophobic, moving in step with a man's wide back in front of me, but Jaxson can see over the crush of people and I count on that and his touch to see me through the crowd.

Before we reach the parking lot, there's a disturbance behind me and his hand falls away. I twist to see, but people urge me forward. I call his name several times, but there's no answer. One guy yells, "I'll be your Jaxson, babe, wait for me at the entrance." Laughter follows, so I keep quiet and walk.

We spill out into the vast parking lot, where people hang out in front of their cars singing the songs from the concert while waiting for the long trail of cars exiting the dusty lot to dwindle.

My phone and wallet are in the sack with Jaxson, so I have no way of contacting anyone. I've never been to Shoreline, and I'm not sure if I'm in the right section where we parked the car.

I lean against an enormous lamp pole assessing my uncertain position, aware some are taking notice of a girl alone, and soon someone will be bold enough to approach me. I scan in all directions looking for someone employed by the venue to help me, but no one is in a neon vest labeled Security, so I head back to the entrance.

Frustrated that I'm left alone in this position, tears streak my cheeks, so I maneuver my way through cars and groups of people because it seems like the logical move. I'm still a distance away, when it's clear the entrance is locked and soon the parking lot will be deserted.

I jog up to the entrance and slam my palm against the gate. If I make enough noise, someone should answer. My pleas to open up motivate a few stragglers to offer help, but they're three drunk guys holding beers, standing off to the side and discussing me.

They look like professional concert goers, the kind that follow the band and discuss the importance of their music ad nauseam. I need to do something before they agree on a plan. I continue banging, keeping an eye on them and wondering if I can outrun three out-of-shape, inebriated males. But where could I go? We're out in something that looks like a cow pasture.

A muffled "Chloe!" sails from behind the drunk trio.

I crane my neck and squint at the darkness, willing it to be Jax, but no one appears. One of the drunk guys is glancing behind him, confirming the sound wasn't in my head.

A short, sturdy-looking guy with glasses rounds the triad, striding between me and my audience.

"Hey, you Chloe?" the newcomer says.

I don't know this guy. I nod and keep them all in my sight, prepared to run.

I must look wild, because he raises a hand motioning 'you need to calm the fuck down.'

"Hey," he calls over his shoulder. "I found her, she's over here."

Heavy footsteps signal another male approach while new guy backs away. A figure jogs out of the darkness.

"Jaxson!" I run at him, knocking him back with force.

"Hey, this your girl, dude? We were trying to help," said the one least intoxicated from the trio. The other two bob their heads, agreeing, but they lose interest in our reunion and move away.

"Yeah, she's mine," he says, cradling me and kissing my hair.

I cry and tighten my grip around his waist, my heart thumping.

"Thanks for finding her, man," he says to the guy with glasses.

"Sure, no problem. You guys take care."

Jaxson glances over at the last guy from the threesome. "Thanks for watching over her."

"No problem," he says, lifting his beer to us, then trails off to catch up with his friends.

Angry fear wells up and I clench fists full of his shirt. "What happened to you? You didn't answer when I called."

"Hey, hey," he soothes. "I didn't do it on purpose. Some guy fell and almost

85

took me down with him. I was lucky I wasn't trampled. You were gone when someone pulled me upright. The crowd took me to the north gate. I've been searching for you."

The fringe of hair in his eyes can't hide his worry.

"Jax, you took my phone," I say, tugging his shirt. "I mean Jaxson," I correct, frustrated.

He smiles. "I'm glad you're safe. It scared the shit out of me when I couldn't find you." He hugs me tighter and I bury my face in his chest, relieved his arms are around me.

"I never let anyone call me Jax, but I like it when you say it."

The breeze carries a scent of sage when Jax pushes away from the railing. "Good, that's settled. There's no reason to be formal when we're alone." He motions me to the small buffet table. "I hope you'll eat something. Brita and I were playing twenty questions yesterday trying to figure out what you would like for breakfast. As usual, she errs on the side of excess." Jax picks up a plate, holding it out as I move toward him.

"Sorry for asking. You can tell me it's none of my business, but why do you have a Band-Aid on your hand and knee?"

I'd changed the dressing this morning after my shower and forgotten about it until this moment. "I was walking in a parking lot that needed repair. My heel got caught on a divot in the asphalt and I took a tumble. My pride was more injured than my hand or my knee. By the way, I'm fine."

"Good, I need you in excellent form," he teases.

I'm caught up in his signature smile until he offers the plate again. I grab it and start peeking under small silver domes to reveal enough food for twenty people. I wasn't in the mood for a breakfast burrito, sausage, eggs, pancakes, or waffles. I think I saw eggs Benedict. I normally just have a cup of coffee in the morning. I was going to unenthusiastically pile food on my plate until I see a slice of heaven sitting in the corner of the buffet. I point. "Is that by any chance homemade?"

Jax glances in the direction. "That's a Brita specialty. I hired her because she makes the best cherry strudel I've ever tasted."

I grab a server to slide a thick slice onto my plate and finish it with a large dollop of whipped cream from a chilled crystal bowl. I sit to enjoy my feast.

Jax throws a few items on his plate and pours coffee. He slides across from me. "Have you thought about my request?"

I've already finished my first bite. He's right about the strudel. I'm thinking about stealing another tiny portion before I answer, or maybe this is the time to discuss that I'm leaving? I grimace at the pastry, knowing that after my announcement, there's no reason to stay. "About that. I think you'll be an amazing councilmember for District 5."

He sets his fork down, watchful.

Now that I've begun, it's harder than I expected. If only things could be different. It would be a dream to help him make his mark on the city.

"I'm sure whatever you choose as your platform will make a positive impact on your constituents. But I won't be a part of it."

He takes a sip of coffee, unfazed by what I've just said. "Has something happened?"

I place my fork beside my plate. It's no use to pretend I'll finish after this conversation. "I've been thinking about this for a long time. I'd planned to leave after Peterson left office. He intended to retire after this last campaign. This would have been his last term. I'm just stepping up my timetable."

He pushes his plate away and inspects the view. "You're leaving the city? Have you got another job offer?"

"No, I'm not leaving the city." I'll be honest, at least part of it isn't a lie. "I've heard the Assistant City Manager position might open. I want a shot at that job. I've spent all my time in District 5. This is a diverse city and I'd like to try working for another district staff with different constituents and new challenges."

"I want the opportunity to change your mind," he says.

I sit back. I'd expected that he would be unhappy, but I didn't think he would try to keep me.

"Have you already talked to somebody about this transfer?"

"I spoke to Arlene yesterday. To be fair, she asked me to give it a week and if I still feel the same, she'll start looking for a new position for me."

He lets that linger for a bit. Only the sound of birds chirping overhead breaks the silence.

"I want big changes for District 5. When I learned we would be working together, I knew you were the best person to help make these changes. I come from business. I'm used to the driving atmosphere of competition, commerce, profit. Did I push you too hard the first day?"

The first day was a disordered mess and I'm still getting calls from the staff trying to calm their fears, but that's always been part of my job.

"No, I'm not afraid of a challenge."

"That's why I need you. We're on the cutting edge of something new. I get that you want diversity in your background, but what I want to do will go well beyond District 5. I plan to impact the entire city."

"I wish it could be different."

"I have a week to change your mind." He sits back, transitioning into CEO mode. "I warn you. I'm used to getting what I want and right now, I want you with me. I suggest we meet here for breakfast every day to work on agendas. Eat your strudel; there's something I want to show you after you finish."

11

Swim Lanes

*J*ax downshifts the red sports car. The convertible hugs the curve as the weight of the speed almost renders me speechless. He glances at me, dark glasses gleaming and the wind streaking through his hair. I swear, he looks like a Hollywood movie star; he looks that perfect in the moment.

"Do you like fast cars?" He shouts to be heard over the competing noise.

I nod, unable to do much more than grit my teeth.

After the last sharp turn, I close my eyes, praying we'll make it safely to the main street. We careen around two more hairpin turns until the Jag slows to idle at the bottom of the hill for the stop sign. He takes a left onto the main road and the ride is less frantic.

He glimpses me for a moment. The tinted lenses of his sunglasses hide his eyes. "I'm making an assumption here, that you want to move on because working with me will be a major shift away from Peterson's management style. I also think not knowing who I am plays a big part in this equation."

He eases the car onto the on-ramp to the freeway. The metering lights are on and we sit, waiting for the light to change. His impatient fingers cradle the stick shift.

"There's more to me than what they print; most of that stuff is exaggerated to sell magazines, newspapers, books, whatever. I'll admit it helps cement my reputation, but no one has come close to getting beyond that hype."

The light blinks green and he accelerates, cutting off more conversation.

I know little about the adult him, other than what I glean from articles I come across. I fell in love with him at first sight, and I'm still dealing with the emotions of a sixteen-year-old where he's concerned. That's why it's important I work this out and get past this teenage obsession.

We pull into the parking lot of Anselm Prep, our old high school. The school is closed. The students haven't returned from the winter holidays. We walk to the front door and we're greeted by a man with thinning gray hair, in dark-blue work clothes with the name David embroidered over the shirt pocket.

"Principal Roberts called and asked me to give you a tour, Councilman Bennett."

"Thanks, this is Chloe Ivarsson, my Chief of Staff."

"I'm David. Glad to meet you, Ms. Ivarsson." He turns his attention back to Jax. "Principal said you wanted to look at the swim pavilion."

When did the pool become a swim pavilion? I look at Jax to ask, but his attention is still on David.

"Follow me," David says, sweeping his hand in the door's direction. "I'm guessing you already know where it is, but I'll still need to open gates and doors for you to get inside."

There was no need for a guide; I've walked this hall several times.

I can still see this corridor filled with laughing students in clusters and inhale the pungent aroma of teenage bodies, bringing me back to a time when this was my world. When we leave the main building to walk across the courtyard, a new structure looms up in front of us.

"The principal said you haven't been here since the groundbreaking. He still says it was a shame that the man who donated the building was out of the country when we opened the place."

Jax keeps his gaze on the structure. "I've been meaning to come by for a few years to see it in person. I've only seen the architect's drawings and the pictures from the opening ceremony."

The pavilion has two swimming pools, an outdoor with viewing stands and its twin, an enclosed structure. It's likely they use the indoor pool for practice, or a second competition venue. We're looking around like two tourists taking in the massive complex.

David pulls a watch from his pocket. "I'll leave you two to wander by yourselves since you were a student here, Councilman Bennett. I'll be in the office. Visit me on your way out."

We walk up a few rows and take seats, looking out at the outdoor facility. I imagine the place bustling with people, students nervous about their race and spectators milling in the stands, watching.

"Why did you donate a swim pavilion to Anselm? I don't recall anything in the news."

He rubs his chin, taking in the blue water below, reluctant to talk now that we're here.

"I donated the building under the condition that I'd be an anonymous donor, although the building is named after my grandfather, Alexander Bennett."

It makes sense. He was a star player on the water polo team. "Why did you feel the need to donate pools to your old high school? Did they approach you as an alumnus to help upgrade this structure?"

"I contacted Principal Roberts about the idea. We worked together on the project until we have what you see today. It was something I'd been thinking about for a while." He glances down at his flexing hands. "Not many people know I was sick most of my childhood, and that meant I was homeschooled. When I graduated from the middle-school curriculum, I begged my mother to let me go to a public high school. She eventually said yes, even though she was afraid for my health."

Pieces fall into place of his life before I met him. I thought because of his money, and that boyish confidence, he always had an easy life.

"Was swimming part of a therapy? Was it something you did as a child?"

He shakes his head. "They never allowed me in our pool. I learned to swim the summer before my freshman year. The list of sports my mother wouldn't let me participate in was long. Imagine telling a kid who dreams of playing football, basketball, or baseball that they're not strong enough to play. It was a battle to find something. I didn't want to be one of those kids who sat in the library all day. When I suggested water polo, she said yes. My freshman year, the water and the practice strengthened my body, and I grew a few inches that summer."

He stares at the pool like he's watching a replay of events. "Swimming was the one thing that changed my life. I thought joining the team would help me be like other kids my age, but I was good at swimming and a few kids on the team were just as good or better and we won games and a state championship."

The recall lights his face and I'm able to glimpse that teenage boy again, but the vision produces a regret that I couldn't help him.

"That small, sickly kid was popular. For the first time, I had friends. You don't know what that's like for a lonely child who just wanted to fit in. This pavilion is a way of giving back. I want other kids to have the same opportunity."

"I remember three other swim pavilions built recently and heard about plans for more, all in high schools. Is that you?"

"Guilty," he says, holding his hands up in mock surrender. It's enough to shift the conversation from the serious past. "This is a private school, and more than likely these students have access to a pool. I want to build more of these in public schools. It will not only encourage water sports and activities, but these venues can be rented out to organizations for added revenue for the school or open for public use. I built the one in Anselm with my own money. After that, I set up a fund through my company."

He pushes to his feet, extending a hand to me. The gesture looks formal, like an invitation to dance. "There's more to see; let's tour the rest of the campus."

I clasp his hand, and he pulls me to my feet. We're standing too close for anyone to think we're just two coworkers on a city tour. I'm looking into his eyes, but what's going through his mind is unclear. I'm caught by the moment, and a shiver passes through me that's a combination of his presence and the lingering cold. My suit's wool jacket is too light for the cold weather. I wrap my arms around myself without thinking.

It breaks the spell when Jax shrugs out of his coat, revealing a navy sweater underneath. Although I'm freezing, I don't understand why he's shedding clothing.

"I've dragged you out in the cold without warning." He slips the heavy jacket onto my shoulders. The wool fills me with his warmth and his scent.

"Aren't you cold?" I say, hoping for something other than his jacket.

He draws the coat tighter around me. "I'm always hot. I would have thrown this jacket in the back of the car soon. Where do you want to go next? Want to see the gym where we held our rallies?"

"The football field," I respond. I should have hesitated with my response, like I'm considering his suggestion, but it slips out quicker and more decisive than I want.

93

His eyes narrow, but he doesn't ask the question. "Sure, it's not far; are you warm enough?"

I turn away from him and begin traversing the steps toward the exit. We arrive at the field a few minutes later and again I'm struck by my memories of the band playing, the cheerleaders shouting at an excited crowd, even the grunts of the players on the field.

"Did you ever come to a football game?" I ask. It's not a chance question. We both spent a lot of time on this field. My most enduring memory is him sitting in the stands with his buddies watching the cheerleaders.

I know he was here for his girlfriend Portia, but I'd pretended he was my boyfriend here to watch me. I'm older, but I don't think I've changed that much.

Jax moves next to me and we look out at the deserted expanse of grass. I'm hoping this will shake loose some memory of me.

"Yeah, a few times." He seems reluctant to talk about it.

I push a little more, hoping to spark something. "Was it difficult to visit the field because you wanted to play football?"

He looks down at me with a sheepish grin that touches my heart. "I told you I was popular. My girlfriend was the head cheerleader. I'd come to watch her." He sighs and looks out again. "That was a long time ago. A lot has happened since then."

I turn away like I'm searching the opposite field to hide the hurt that's erasing the hopes I had of this place reminding him of me. The wind whips up, sending a new wave of cold. I wrap my arms about myself, not for warmth, but for comfort.

"You're swimming in that coat," he says. "I think you should put it on instead of wearing it like a cape." He's pushing it off my shoulders and helps me into the sleeves. I fumble with the buttons.

"I'll do the buttons," he says. "Put your hands in the pockets to keep them warm."

His deft fingers travel up my front, securing each button in place until he flips the collar and closes the button near my throat. It's too big for me. There's a large gap around my neck, but my arms are toasty. The attention and closeness to him is unbearable. I want to touch him, drag my fingers through his hair, and taste his lips to know it's him. He leans into me close enough for a kiss, but he's slipping his arm under mine.

"I think we've seen enough of the campus. Let's get you back to the car and I'll turn up the heater."

Jax opens the door for me. He put the sports car's top up before our tour. I slip inside the small space, grateful to be out of the wind. Before Jax opens the driver's door, his phone rings. He leans against the side of the car and has a brief conversation, then climbs in and drops his phone into the cupholder.

"That was Bruce, my assistant," he says, distracted. "You two should have met during breakfast, but why that didn't happen is another story. I've asked Bruce to make lunch reservations for us at my favorite restaurant."

"But lunch is hours away."

Jax throws his arm around the back of my seat and leans in close enough for his hazel eyes to meet mine. "Ivarsson, haven't you figured out yet that we're spending the day together?"

12

Time of Our Lives

We ditch the car at the San Mateo Bart station and ride the crowded train into San Francisco. It's only a short walk from the Embarcadero to the Ferry building. While we trudge down the hill, Jax offers to buy me a coat, arguing it's his fault that I'm cold because he didn't consider the weather when he asked me to come with him on this last-minute trip.

I brush off the suggestion with a half sigh. I make up the excuse that I already have too many jackets in my closet and what would be the sense of adding another? It stops his banter, so I'm guessing he's not satisfied with my answer. I know I look odd swallowed up in a man's huge coat, but it feels cozy, like a continuous warm hug from him.

"That was seriously the best meal I've ever had," I say as Jax helps me into his coat in front of the hostess podium. We stand among a large press of bodies filling the small waiting area in the restaurant. Their voices blend into a loud murmur while they cluster in groups, waiting for the hostess to acknowledge their presence. I nearly bump into a woman who's come up beside me. She places a light hand on my arm.

"You know, love," she leans in, her British cadence charming. "I'd wear my husband's coat when I was too far along in my pregnancy."

Maybe this cute grandmother can't see that well. I nod to acknowledge her, but she tugs at my sleeve, wanting more of my attention.

"When is your baby due?" she whispers.

I might embarrass her with a denial. When I don't answer, the woman turns a pleading face to Jax. He surprises me when he slips a possessive arm around my shoulders, drawing me to him.

"She's not allowed to have the baby until she marries me first," he says with a straight face.

The woman gives him a sad smile and pats his arm. "Well, you should have gotten that buy-in first. Nature's not going to wait for you two. I suggest you settle your differences and think of a name."

"That's good advice, ma'am, thank you," Jax says with a formality I've never heard from him nor expected. He finishes off the deception with a that's settled look at me and a squeeze.

My teeth clamp down on the inside of my cheek as the sweet woman moves past us, heading further into the restaurant and shaking her head. We escape in the opposite direction to the brisk outside. I break away from Jax when we're out on the pavement and fall into a fit of giggles.

He considers me, not understanding what's obvious to me.

"Why are you laughing? What else was I going to say to that nice woman?" A corner of his mouth moves south. "You don't think it's possible that we could have a baby?"

I do a laugh hiccup, starting a fresh round of giggles that has me struggling to talk. "What I can't see, is Jaxson Bennett, the Valley's sexy capitalist, with a child."

He looks down at me, his dimples making an appearance. "You think I'm sexy?"

"Please," I say and wave him away, "you know what you look like. Weren't you voted the sexiest CEO in Silicon Valley last year?"

He throws a look down the street, avoiding my scrutiny. "It wasn't much of a competition. I didn't know I was in the running until they sent me the issue." He turns back to me with seriousness that stops my teasing. "If you want to be leered at and hounded relentlessly, be named the sexiest anything and watch your life change."

I shrug, not believing he didn't like some part of the limelight.

"Come on, Ivarsson, that's not me. I don't strut around with my shirt open to my navel like a privileged rock star. I'm just a guy; don't believe my press."

I've dealt enough with the press to know what they write isn't all true…who'd want to read about a dull CEO? I was with Jax before his Silicon Valley fame, when he was a teenager with a crooked smile, brushing his too-long hair from his eyes when he talked. I fell in love with that version of him and wanting him has never stopped.

We're blocks away from the Ferry building. San Francisco is a gray cold with a little fog rolling off the ocean. It's been raining off and on since we arrived.

We join other tourists heading toward Pier 39 and duck inside shops when the rain comes down in short bursts. Jax has enough of dodging the raindrops. At the next tourist shop we shelter in, he buys two red umbrellas that say: I heart San Francisco. We mill around the small store for a bit together and separately look at souvenirs, waiting for the weather to change.

San Francisco is only forty-five miles from the South Bay, which is Silicon Valley. The San Francisco area is North Bay and Oakland, Berkeley is the East Bay. The west, well that's the ocean, so there's lots to see and do in this portion of California. Jax slips behind me as I'm looking at a leather bracelet. It's cute, but the city's name is on everything.

"See anything you like?"

"No, I'm good," I say, placing the bracelet back in the bin.

"Are you ready to head out?"

We walk outside under the awning, stopping short to push open our umbrellas in time for another burst of rain. "Could you wait here? I think I left something," Jax says.

Before I can ask what, he slips back into the shop. I lean against the building, waiting, watching rain-soaked people. For lack of anything else to do, I pull out my lipstick and touch up the color. He appears when I drop the lipstick back in my bag.

Jax attempts to reopen his umbrella, struggling with the button until it pops open. "I thought I'd left my card. I couldn't remember if I'd gotten it back from him. The guy was nice enough to check the floor, but I found it stuck in the wrong slot in my wallet." He looks down the street. "We can walk to Ghirardelli Square from here or we can find a ride to Chinatown or North Beach."

I'm scanning the same landscape, deciding which of the choices would be more interesting, when something catches my eye across the street. "There's a gelato shop over there." I don't wait for a response. I grab Jax's hand, wait for a break in the traffic, and pull him to safety on the other side of the road. We're standing in front of Calliope's Gelato, and my nose is almost pressed against the window of the busy shop.

"You can't tell me you're still hungry, Ivarsson? Didn't I feed you enough at the restaurant?"

I ignore him and push my way into the shop. He follows me and I inspect the colorful selection of frozen cream.

"Would you like to have a taste, Miss?" says a friendly attendant.

"I'll have a taste of the pistachio." She produces the sample and I take the baby-size plastic spoon from her. The flavor is like warm, sweet roasted nuts. I smile at Jax with the spoon still in my mouth. I pull it out, pointing it at him. "First, we didn't have dessert at lunch. Second, there's always room for gelato." I turn back to the case, deciding to taste something different. "This is my treat, Jax; what will you have?"

He stands to the side of me, arms folded, not happy with this unexpected turn. He's a planner. This trip might appear spontaneous, but I know Jax had it planned out in his head how he wants each part of this day trip to happen. He likes desserts as much as I do, and he probably planned something high-end and exclusive, like a chocolate wine tasting.

"I asked you to spend the day with me. If anyone is treating, it would be me." He looks at the expectant attendant. "Give her whatever she wants, and I'll have a double rocky road."

"I'll have one scoop of the pistachio," I say. I won't argue if he's paying.

The attendant's hand hovers above the containers. "Cup or cone?"

"Cone," I say.

"Cup for me," Jax says.

We take a seat in the corner of the small shop with our treats. A couple of adults with lively kids have just left. The shop quiets and soft background music gives us an opportunity to talk.

He stares down at the cup of frozen chocolate. "You're lucky it's about 80° in here. Having ice cream outside in this cold rain would be a challenge."

I take a lick of my gelato and savor the taste. "Why are we here in San Francisco? I thought you'd show me more of your life in the valley after we toured the Anselm campus."

He pushes a spoon in his cup. "Did you want to see the house where I grew up or the bar where me and my buddies from school conceived my company? I can still take you to those places."

"I want to know what's important to the real you, not the hype in your bio." It slips out unguarded, but I want to push Jaxson out of the way and talk to my Jax.

Mild surprise squints his eyes.

Maybe that revealed too much of my feelings. We're silent for a few moments while I tune back into the shop's background noise to think.

He gives a distracted laugh. "I thought showing you the place that changed my life would tell you more about me than what came after."

"Is this your plan? That a campus tour of your old high school and an amazing meal in San Francisco will convince me to continue working for you?"

He breathes out a frustrated sigh. "Let's agree not to talk about you leaving the team and no shop talk. Can't we be two people enjoying a day out?"

The whole thing hits me wrong and I stop my eating. I can't pretend we're just two people out on a day trip. This frustrating charade gets harder to maintain when only one of us knows we have a past.

I look down at gelato streaking my thumb. I catch it with a couple of strategic licks, finishing with my thumb in my mouth to remove anything I missed.

Jax stirs in his seat, watching me. "You're really enjoying that."

I shrug. "What can I say? I like ice cream." Then I notice I need to eat more and talk less.

I'm almost down to the cone, which is my second favorite part. I continue to lick with a little more enthusiasm.

"You know you're distracting when you do that." He glances toward the counter.

All I wanted was an Italian gelato, but I'd forgotten how difficult it is for me to eat an ice cream and keep a conversation going. He looks back as I take a lick. This time I meet his eyes. He's staring at my mouth.

I take another lick, slower this time, to test my hunch. He doesn't turn away and I see it. His mouth parts slightly and there's no mistaking the absolute craving in his eyes. He's mesmerized by my bright pink lips on a creamy green surface.

Awareness blinks his eyes, and he pulls his gaze from me. "I'm done with my gelato," he rasps. He can't look at me as he pushes the chair away. "I'll wait for you outside."

Maybe some muscle memory of our connection is kicking in. I let out a breath. I can't afford to hope that he remembers. I adjust my coat and prepare for another disappointment. Reluctantly, I deposit my cone in the bin on my way out. Jax leans against the shop, jaw tight, distracted. He says nothing, just begins walking.

"What's wrong?"

"Nothing."

"It can't be nothing."

We're silent, walking toward Ghirardelli Square. We cross the street, heading up an open path. There's an icy drizzle as I catch his hand.

"Talk to me," I whisper.

He looks ahead, determined to keep walking, but he doesn't release my hand. "You work for me, Ivarsson, it's not right," he mumbles, but he won't say more.

I glance up the lane to the open mall that's still a few minutes' walk away. This time of day and with the weather the way it is, it's almost deserted. The rain is starting again in fat drops. Cars splash through the water down below on the street. Jax halts and I nearly stumble my step.

"We forgot our umbrellas. Go up the path...you can make it

before the rain gets worse. I'll get them. Stay near the entrance. I'll look for you there."

My stomach twists when his hand slips from mine. This sudden feeling of loss scares me. He turns to stride down the path. I want to go with him, but I'm helpless to move.

The sky releases a heavy burst. "Don't leave," I call out to his retreating back. The water beating the pavement drowns out my plea. Not again. He can't leave me again.

He turns back, blinking the droplets from his eyes, straining to hear. "What, what did you say?" he shouts back.

Cold water slides down my hair in rivulets, seeping inside the collar of my coat. The wet cold finds my light clothing underneath, stealing my warmth. The sense of losing him deepens when his scent is erased by the soaked wool.

How can I convince myself he's not leaving me again? I stretch out my hand. "Don't go, Jax, stay with me."

He observes me but makes no move to return. I must be a pleading mess, a scared, washed-out version holding out my palm as the hard rain cascades down on us.

His frustrated hand wipes the rain from his eyes, but water continues to drip from his face.

He comes back, his arms about me, my body held against his chest. I stand on my toes, wanting to be level with his face, cursing that this would be easier if I were taller. My fingers find his collar, and with all my strength I pull him to me. He doesn't budge, just stares at me, uncertain. He can't be that oblivious to what I want. I need his kiss like it's my salvation, but he continues to search my face.

It's crazy to be here in the middle of a public place with rain beating down on us. I grip his collar tighter until the resistance leaves his body. Our lips press together, hard and hungry to sustain this moment. I melt into his kiss. The thought of everything slides away to the chocolate taste of his lips and the roar of water in my ears. Maybe somewhere inside him he's remembering me. "Jax," I sigh into his mouth and I'm shaking.

Jax's hands cradle my face, ending our kiss. "I need to get you out of this rain," he shouts in my face.

I nod, ready to follow him away from here. He finds my hand and leads me down to the street.

Cars swish down the road in the blinding rain. Jax tries to hail a cab for two drenched people, but no one stops. They're probably afraid of the damage we'll do to their backseats.

Cold seeps into my bones from the water that continues to find its way under my coat. My shaking is like uncontrollable tremors.

Jax abandons my hand to place an arm around me, as he moves us almost in the line of traffic to frantically wave at cars. A cab pulls near us and stops. Jax opens the door and pushes me inside.

"Thanks for picking us up. I'll pay for any damage to your car."

"Sounds good to me…where are you going?"

"The Maxwell."

"Okay." He pulls the car out into traffic. "The Max it is."

I lay across Jax's lap, holding onto myself while he makes a call.

"Yes, I'm on my way now. Have the room ready and tell them to crank up the heat and draw a bath. Could you brew coffee? Is Angela working today? Ask her to send up a catalog. Thank you, I'll see you soon."

He clicks off. The heat in the cab is on, but the coat's heavy, soppy wetness makes me feel worse.

Jax smooths matted strands from my face. "We're not far away from the Max," he says with worried assurance. "I'll take care of you; I promise you'll be comfortable soon."

13

Lightning Before the Thunder

ax's arm is around me when we burst into the lobby of the Max. I'm holding onto his waist, a fist full of his soggy sweater bunching in my hand. A man rushes up to us with two people trailing behind him. "Mr. Bennett, I'm Kevin Rosco, the senior ambassador at the Maxwell. Your accommodations are ready, if you will follow me." He waves his reluctant assistants away to places behind a desk.

We trail behind him through the lobby, not even getting a curious eye from the people walking through. Nothing alarms anyone in a big city; people are too busy with their own lives to care.

We continue our trek and all I can think about is a warm, dry bathrobe at the end of this walk. We skirt a bank of elevators to one designated for the upper floors. Kevin swipes his key card, then motions us in when the doors open. He steps inside, punching a button, keeping his back to us. The door closes and my stomach fights to exit my body as we swiftly travel upward. The dark elevator gives way to gray light as the landscape of the city fans out before us.

"Sorry this isn't a better day to see the view, but San Francisco is beautiful no matter when you see her," he says, keeping his eyes glued to the panel. I look down at my feet, aware that the wet wool is pungent in this small space; my only solace is me clinging to Jax's solid form.

The elevator chimes, and the door opens into a spacious living room. I glimpse my surroundings, aware we just stepped off a private elevator into a penthouse suite with a panoramic view of downtown San Francisco.

"Everything you requested is here. The master bedroom is to the right and guest bedrooms to the left. You'll find robes and slippers in all bathrooms. Is there anything else I can do for you?"

"No, thank you," Jax says.

"If you need your clothes laundered, call me I'll have them picked up and serviced while you wait."

Kevin leaves us standing in the living room as the elevator doors close. I turn away to inspect the view, shy after our kiss on the path.

"Use the master bedroom," Jax suggests, "I'll be in the guest bedroom. When you feel better, come back here and we can figure out the clothes."

The bathroom is a shrine to luxury in smoky gray marble and glass. The steamy warmth of the bath has me letting go of some of my anxiety. I pick a jar of bath salts from a selection on a shelf. I dump in crystals and watch them dissolve while I shed my heavy wet clothes. I sink into the deep tub until the purple water is to my chin. I lean back, sigh, and bask in the lavender-scented water.

Jax has chosen soft, classical music to fill the silent space. Edvard Grieg's *Concerto in A Minor* drifts around me as the waters restore my body. I think of Jax in the rain holding me, desperate to connect through that kiss. I don't know what it meant to him or what he might think of me, because that kiss was my idea.

I'm not surprised Jax brought me to a place above the city. He enjoys gazing into the evening sky as the sun sets. It's likely why he chose to live in the hills.

Our first date was on the roof of the Almaden residence tower in downtown San Pacitas before its official opening. They landscaped the rooftop like a garden with a section for outdoor dining for large parties and smaller intimate alcoves for smaller groups. The view to the west was a section of the old city that had Spanish California-style buildings mixed with their more modern cousins that tapered off near the mountains.

Jax asked me to attend an '80s film festival in an old movie house in Palo Alto, but he wanted to do a quick detour to see a new building he'd read about. He confessed later that he was afraid I'd think he was uncool to invite me to watch the sunset instead of exploring his interest in architecture. Jax didn't know that if he'd suggested attending a clown convention, I'd have happily donned a red nose and had my face painted white.

Remembering back, that first sunset-gazing almost didn't happen. I got back to my dorm room late after my last class, and the building's security was on a break when we arrived. We walked from the elevator onto the roof as the sun was setting. Jax said the guy who led us up to the roof was an old friend, but I saw him slip him money when he thanked him.

He pulled two chairs to an observation point, but we didn't use them. We leaned against the railing, elbows resting, watching the colors of evening enveloped by the colors of night. At the last of twilight time, Jax placed his arm around my shoulders and I leaned into him.

We'd never kissed before. We'd talked; long, drawn-out

conversations in my dorm room, both of us leaning against the headboard. I always seemed to have my knees to my chest, my arms wrapped around my legs, watching an animated Jax talk about everything with passion. It's not like I didn't want to kiss him. All I thought about when we were together was imagining what it would be like. In those first days in my room, it never seemed to be the right time; it was all too new for both of us.

What happened on that roof is still a sweet memory. It was just Jax, me, and a night full of stars. He leaned over, hesitated for a heartbeat, and then we shared the most amazing kiss. I wanted to stay on that rooftop all night under the stars, but he said we were only allowed to be up here for an hour. He had brought me here because he wanted us to be somewhere special for our first kiss.

I push my toe out of the water and engage the hot tap. I've been soaking for nearly an hour. The hot water spills into the cooling tub and I do a swimming motion to circulate the warmth. Light tapping at the door has me reaching for the tap to turn it off.

"Are you okay in there? Do you need anything?" Jax's muffled voice doesn't hide his concern.

I'm not sure I want to see him yet. "I'm fine. Thank you for asking them to draw a bath. I'm almost 100%."

He doesn't respond.

"Jax, are you still there?"

A few seconds later, I hear him dragging something heavy to the door. I realize it's a chair when I hear the creak of leather.

"I think our day together is turning to shit," he says. I can see his frown even with the closed door between us.

"You shouldn't be so hard on yourself; rain is a good thing in

California," I shout at the door. "And I wouldn't call taking a bath at the Max the worst thing that's ever happened to me."

He chuckles. "You're right, the shower I just took was pretty amazing, but you know what I'm talking about."

I push out of the tub dripping on the bathmat, reaching for an extra-fluffy towel on the warmer.

"Ivarsson, I've been attracted to you since we met," he says, the seriousness returning to his voice. "I tried to keep my feelings to myself…"

This reminds me of a penitent confessing his sins to a priest in a confessional. The door is like a curtain that separates the sinner from the absolver.

"I thought I'd gotten it under control at the gelato shop, but I caved when we were on the path to the square."

I finger-comb my damp hair, wishing I could put it into a ponytail. I take the silk bathrobe from the hook. Checking my image in the mirror, I adjust my sash. Every piece of water-soaked clothing I walked in wearing is in a neat pile in the corner. I swing the door open to a surprised Jax. "I kissed you, or don't you remember that?"

Jax takes in my rejuvenated form. He scrambles to his feet, regaining control. He appears more severe with wet blonde hair slicked back in a black robe that's gaped open to reveal a portion of his broad chest.

"You shouldn't need to put up with my attention." He seems anxious to make whatever sin he thinks he's committed against me right. "I'm the boss; it's not right to put you in that position. It won't happen again if you agree to stay, but if you decide to leave, I won't oppose your transfer."

I want to explore what's underneath that robe, run my hand along the planes of his body. Instead, I push past him, avoiding his boring chivalry. "I smell coffee. I need a cup."

"Sure, they brewed some, it's on the counter. If you want a latte, they have a machine."

The dark wood and black counter kitchen is large and well stocked. I hunt around for cups and pull out two.

"Do you want coffee?"

"Yeah, I'll have some," he says, watching me move around the kitchen. "Where did you leave your clothes? They'll be here soon to collect them."

"In the bathroom." I gesture with the pot.

Jax returns with a bag as a maid enters the living room. He hands her the sack.

"We'll call when its ready, Mr. Bennett. I have a message to give you from Angela. She can send up anything you like…just give her the sizes. She left a card to fill out in the sample catalog or call her."

"Thank you."

Jax slips onto the stool at the counter as the maid disappears into the elevator. "Before you ask who Angela is, she's a personal stylist employed by the Max. It might be awhile before our clothes are ready. I've asked her to send some things up for me. I feel responsible for what happened. I've asked her to shop for you; she's just waiting for your sizes. Order anything you like; I'll take care of it."

I slide Jax's coffee toward him and dump cream into my cup. "It shouldn't take more than an hour for them to service our clothes." Or is he uncomfortable with me only in a robe?

He spoons a lot of sugar in his coffee. "I was going to suggest we return home after visiting Ghirardelli Square, but I'm thinking a change of plans. There's lots to do in San Francisco, but if we go back to the South Bay now, we'll be sitting in traffic for hours."

I take a sip of my coffee. This will give me more alone time with him, maybe another chance that he might remember our past.

"Angela can even pull designer clothes. She'll find anything you ask for." Both his dimples make an appearance. "Think of this as part of our day out."

He doesn't understand that dressing up in designer clothes isn't an incentive for me. I can buy anything Angela has to offer.

My mom is just as wealthy as the Bennetts. My family struggled until my parents divorced and Mom took over the finances. Her psychic counseling business exploded, and it just keeps growing. I've got a healthy trust fund that I rarely touch. I appear middle class with my Japanese sedan and clothes from Talbots, because I didn't grow up wealthy. I like who I am; things don't matter to me.

"Hmm, designer clothes, you say?"

He perks up at my response. "I would feel better if you'd say yes."

He wants to play *My Fair Lady*, the movie where a snooty professor turns a street urchin into a lady. They fall in love at the end. So, yeah, I'll be his Eliza Doolittle. "Okay, if I can talk to her. I want to make sure she understands my style."

He hands me a card.

I snatch it from him and pick up my cup. "I'll talk to her in the bedroom. I assume I can continue to use the master bedroom?"

He nods. "Call her now. She's been waiting since we arrived."

I walk toward the master bedroom, taking a sip of coffee while holding the card above my head.

113

14

Room with a View

Fifteen minutes later, two clothing racks appear in the living room. Angela and two male assistants in black bustle into the space. A small woman with oversize black glasses attached to a gold chain and short bobbed hair holds out arthritic fingers covered with rings.

"You must be Chloe. I'm Angela." She glances at Jax while we shake hands. "I'm sure Jaxson has told you about me and my service. Jeffrey gave me all your information from your conversation with him." She turns to her assistants. "That's Jeffrey on the right and the other handsome gentleman is Harris. Where can we have a private consultation?"

"The master bedroom," I say.

"Follow me, Jeffrey." The man pushes a rack forward. Angela slips her arm under mine. "Jeffrey will not be in the fitting. The men will assist Jaxson. You know, you're the perfect size for the clothes I pulled for you."

The Angela whirlwind finally leaves, and I'm left with a pile of clothes on the bed that fit perfectly. I'll let Jax buy me an outfit, but I told Angela I would purchase the rest. She's excited to recruit a new client from one of Jax's friends. No more online buying for me after meeting Angela. Next time she promised to come to the South Bay for our next consultation.

"Ivarsson, are you decent?" Jax says to me on the other side of the door. "I thought we could go for dinner upstairs in an hour. If you've never been, we'll have an outrageous view of the entire city, and the food is fantastic."

"Sure, I'll be ready by then."

"Are you coming out here in the meantime? We can talk and discuss what to do after dinner."

He sounds hopeful, but I don't want to see him…not yet. I'm still pissed at him for denying his feelings and pushing me away because of some kind of screwed-up code of ethics.

"I'm kind of tired," I call back. "I'm going to take a nap, then get ready. Whatever you want to do after dinner is fine with me."

He's silent, standing next to the door. "Okay, I'll see you in the living room in an hour."

The hour is not enough time to unwind, but I'm able to pull it together and appear on time as promised. The lights are soft when I enter the living room. Jax stands in front of the view, hands in pockets. He's changed the music to soft jazz, setting a mood that's relaxing, but still upbeat. There's a bottle of wine chilling with two glasses on the counter.

"Is this appropriate for the top of the Max?" I say to announce my presence.

Jax turns.

I take a twirl in my black, sleeveless, cinched-waist circle dress, balancing on red heels. The appreciation that sparks in his eyes as his gaze rakes me from head to toe is the reaction I wanted.

116

"You look beautiful, Ivarsson."

I give him the same brazen appraisal. The dark suit he's wearing is custom. It's hard not to look perfect in a $4,000 suit.

"Thank you, and Mr. Bennett, you look handsome tonight." I receive a shy grin that's a throwback from our time together. I'm surprised he still has that smile in his arsenal.

He strides to the counter and plucks the bottle from the chilling bucket. "I've ordered wine," he says, squinting at the label. "This is a light Tempranillo from Spain. The sommelier I spoke to earlier suggested this as a pre-dinner drink."

Light from the window floods the living room in an unnatural golden radiance as the sun dies into twilight, and it gives Jax a dreamlike quality as he pours. He comes up beside me, handing me a glass. I take the goblet and make an expansive gesture at San Francisco. "This view was worth getting caught in the rain. I could live here all my life and never get used to this place. Do you stay here often?"

"I'm glad I could salvage something out of this day for you, even if it's sharing a drink and admiring a city." He takes a drink and stares at his glass. "I'd use this place for meetings, entertaining clients, sometimes I'd come here to recharge."

We're silent, entertaining our own thoughts for a few long moments. His attention comes back to me when I tug his glass away to place them both on a side table. I know this is risky, but the timing feels right. My hands run up along the front of his jacket to around his neck. Our eyes meet as I become lost in his gaze. My lips brush his with a feather-light kiss.

Jax exhales a ragged breath as his "no" escapes. He captures my arms, pulling them away. I'm puzzled by his reaction. I know he wants me; I can feel he wants me. We were just in the wrong place before.

He's still close, his face meshed in a bewildered annoyance. "We talked about this, Ivarsson. I overstepped last time; this isn't happening again." He turns away, but I feel I'm losing the moment.

117

I don't allow him to retreat; he needs to stay, so I can make him understand I want him. I move forward to square off with him. "You talked and didn't ask me. Don't you think you should ask before you make a decision that affects us both?"

This sparks a reaction, but not what I'd hoped for. "What do you want, because I'm confused? You come to breakfast to give me a half-ass excuse that you don't want to work with me, because you need more diversity. You decide without consulting me, then you kiss me on the path."

The weight of his gaze is on me, waiting for an explanation. I make a quick assessment of how much to reveal; it's not the time for confessions about the past.

"What I said was true. I need to broaden my experience if I want to work in the City Manager's office. It's been my goal for a long time, but it has nothing to do with my attraction to you."

I don't get a *I can't believe you feel the same* vibe from him. If anything, he appears more frustrated. I go on, not waiting for a response. "I thought it might be awkward between us. I didn't know if you felt the same, or if you saw me as one of your groupies that hangs on your godlike words."

Tension runs along his shoulders. "What the fuck, Ivarsson, a groupie? You're my Chief of Staff, not some mindless cult follower." His patience hovers at the edge. "Look, seeing somebody you work with is not a good idea. We're not two anonymous people in a tech company. We work for a very public entity."

His rejection hits me like a fist in the gut. My flight instinct kicks in and I'm thinking how to get away from here, from this pain that's growing bigger.

"It's not right. I'm your boss." The reply softens his reason with regret. "It will look like I've taken advantage of you...used my power to get you in bed." He steps closer, his fingers walking along my hand until it's nestled in his. "Things would get ugly. You could end up disappointed, not to mention the impact to your reputation."

I squeeze his hand, willing him to understand. "Part of my job is assessing risk. I understand what this means and I'm…" I place an emphasis on "I'm" because I want him to know this is not a decision made in the moment. "And I'm willing to take this risk for us."

He eases away from my hand, and I fight the urge to stop its retreat. "I'm sorry, but we can't do this. I didn't mean to mislead you."

This opportunity is slipping away. He's distancing himself, and soon that will be a physical distance as well. I have to do something to stop the ache I've had all these years for him. If this ends here with nothing, I'll never get him out of my heart or my head. I extend my hand. "I want you more, and I'm willing to gamble."

He shakes his head. "Christ, I'm not ready for this. I didn't suggest this outing to seduce you."

That's it, this is the last-ditch effort. I stomp to the counter for my purse, dump the contents on the surface, extract a packet, and throw it at him. He catches it in mid-arc. It's a bold move, but if this doesn't change his mind…at least it will get his attention. He'll know I'm serious.

He examines the packet, turning it over in his palm, then glances back at the bedroom. "Where did you get these?"

"Angela. They came with the clothes she brought. You said she would bring me anything I asked for."

He studies the condoms in his hand, weighing options.

"It's your choice. I can't make my commitment to you any clearer," I say.

There's a painful longing in his eyes that has him fighting against what he wants. He could still say no and this will be over. I just hope tonight he crosses the Rubicon.

He searches the packet as if the answers are written somewhere in the directions. He speaks without taking his gaze from his hands. "It's up to you if you stay on my staff or leave. I won't pressure you to stay with me. But this." He holds up the deciding factor. "If I say yes, we do this once, and there're no repeats."

Unexpected hope lurches in my heart. This might be the only chance I have to kill this demon inside of me that's sapped much of my life away because that door wouldn't close on this man. "I'll take it," I rasp out a whisper. I don't wait for his yes; proposing terms was already an agreement. I take a few steps forward, then launch myself at him.

Jax drops the packet and scoops me up into a kiss. My arms around his neck, I hold on tight to the man I've only dreamed about loving again. He's so goddamn real in my arms that my head spins and I can barely breathe for wanting him.

"I've been waiting for this...you," he says, walking me back into the living room.

It feels like I've won a victory, not the forever and always, but it's a beginning. Jax runs his hands down my sides until one hand finds the hem of my dress. It slips under a light petticoat, creeping the fabric up until his hot hand brushes the curve of my hip. I close my eyes and moan into his mouth. "Let's do it here," I whisper.

He's too intent to shift him to the bedroom, at least not until he's had his fill of exploring. His hand covers my breasts, fingers pinch, rolling my nipple through the fabric until it is a hard pebble.

I'm holding on to the tense muscles of his arms, enjoying the pleasure his palm produces. The sensation halts for only the time it takes for him to slide his palm inside my low neckline to cover my breast, then his fingers grope across my chest. He stiffens, pushes the hand at my hip over my ass, then stops our kiss. "You have nothing underneath this dress," he breathes.

I hold his hand in place to prevent him from moving away from me.

He doesn't resist, but he's not resuming his attention. "The condoms, this?" He squeezes my breast. "Is it all part of a plan?"

Then his hand slips away despite my efforts to keep it close.

I run my hand up his arm to reignite what we had a few moments ago. "That kiss on the path meant something," I remind him to keep his focus on his promise. "You felt it too."

He's rattled that I'm not what he expected. Jax was always affable and charming, but I'd forgotten about the little green control freak he has lurking inside. I'm not seventeen, but I admit I'm surprised at what I'm willing to do to bring him back to me. It's been frustrating; he's like a thread that I can't get to the end of for my prize.

"Jax, it's a bra and panties," I say, leaning my back against the window. "I'd forgotten to ask Angela for underwear. What I wore here wasn't appropriate for this dress," I lie.

He comes back with an unconvinced glare. "That's the story you're sticking with? You remembered condoms, but no underwear?"

I try to look as innocent as possible, but at some point in the evening, I wanted him to know I had nothing on underneath.

Jax moves away, leaving me at the window. He removes his jacket and tie, pitching them at the couch. He swipes the wine bottle and laces two glasses in his fingers. He takes a seat on the floor, the view at his back.

"Jax," I say, moving to take a seat beside him.

"Don't move, sweetheart, you're striking in this light."

The city has dissolved into twilight. The light inside the penthouse is soft. I can still see into the floors of an office building to the right. A man sits alone at a desk in a corner office, shirt sleeves rolled to the elbows. He looks up from his screen to catch me staring. He gives me a nod.

Jax drains his drink, then points his glass at me. "Take off your dress."

"I'm in front of a window. You can't—"

He retrieves the bottle and tops off my glass sitting beside him. He offers it to me, but I motion no.

"I know this." He sighs this out. "You obviously want to seduce me, then do it. Unzip your dress to your waist."

This is my sexy reunion going south. I change my mind and reach for my wine. The sip I take is not for courage, but for time to think.

Jax is waiting for me to fulfill his request; his body is relaxed, eyes lustful as a cat. I remember enough of the old Jax to know he's betting I won't go through with it. This is him taking control. He wants this, and he wants me. I have no choice but to give him a sexy fantasy or take the clothes I bought, call a car, and walk out.

I set the glass down, take my place at the window, my back to Jax. I glance over my shoulder. "Whatever you desire, my prince."

He responds with a low, seductive chuckle, then pulls one leg up to rest his arm on his knee, the wine glass dangling loosely in his hand.

The music changes to something sexier, and I sway my hips to a sultry sax. I draw my fingers to my hair to twist the long length to my front so he has a clear view as I ease the zipper down, stopping at my waist to build his anticipation, but I'm surprised at my own arousal.

I glance beyond Jax to the man in the corner office. He looks like an overachiever, a young executive type, fit, probably a runner or a cyclist. He's moved his chair in front of his desk, watching.

I expose a shoulder while my hand holds my dress front. I try not to focus on the man outside watching me, but my heart races, imagining I'll strip for both men.

"Don't stop. I want to see it all," he urges and takes another drink.

I uncover the second shoulder and let the dress front drop. It stops at my waist, adding a weird layer of fabric to my hips. I don't turn for Jax to see. I push my hair back and peek over at the young exec, wondering what he thinks of this strip show. It's true that people can communicate more deeply with just a look or gesture. He appears to understand what I want from him, and he sits back and nods his appreciation. I wait a few seconds longer to hide my labored breathing.

"Face me, sweetheart."

It's enough encouragement to turn, lace my hands in back of me, tilt my chin up, and face Jax, and the silent participant in this unreality.

"You're a beautiful topless ballerina," he says, referring to the skirt that flounces out from the light petticoat underneath the dress. He takes a drink, his gaze raking my body.

I stare back, daring him to take what he wants.

"Remove it all," he says.

Who's this woman that is turned on by her role in this fantasy with two men? I slide the zipper the rest of the way, giving a little tug to the fabric at my waist. The dress flounces to the floor, pooling at my feet. I kick the garment away. I straighten my back to lift my breasts higher. I remember I need to discard my shoes. I bend at the waist, ready to ease my heels off.

"Keep your heels on."

I stand to my full height, staring ahead at the stranger.

Jax takes his empty glass and places it on the small side table. He twists back to resume his place, looking up at me. "Show me how you play with yourself. I want to see what you do when you're alone."

I toss my head back to get the hair out of my eyes and slide both hands under each breast, lifting and swirling over my mounds. I get a moan from Jax as though he's touching me, and the sound urges me to feel more. I lick my forefingers and place them on my nipples; I pinch and massage, keeping my gaze on Jax, but also beyond him into the night. The man in the corner office has his cock in his hand, stroking it to the rhythm of my pleasure. Jax's back is to the window and doesn't realize there's a voyeur in a fantasy that's not strictly his.

I slide a hand down to touch my wet, swollen clit and imagine Jax's tongue there, his eager mouth tasting me. I close my eyes, lost in my imagination.

123

Jax gets to his feet to stand in back of me, and the soft cotton of his shirt brushes my back. I press hard against him, feeling his cock growing at my back. His hand is at my breast, playing with my nipple. I sigh softly, grinding my butt into him.

"God, you're fucking sexy," he moans into my neck. "How could I want anyone more than you?"

I don't answer. I can't. I won't disturb the dream of him with me, not when I feel like this.

Jax nudges me to the window, placing my hands on the glass above my head. He trails kisses from my neck to the small of my back and caresses my ass before his touch leaves me. I watch his reflection removing his shirt, pants, everything until he brushes my ass with his erection. He pulls me at the waist to bring me a little closer to him, then kicks my legs wider apart. One hand at my breast, he pinches and kneads my nipple, while his finger slides into my wet pussy. His finger flows in and out until he's teased four fingers inside my folds. He fucks me with his fingers as if his cock is inside me and I mew, craving what's to come.

He latches onto my hips, the tip of his cock bumping at my entrance. I'm relaxing as much as my anxious body will allow, knowing his thick cock will spread me to take him in. His first thrust is hard, but by the second I've accepted all of him.

I gasp at the pleasure, unable to catch my breath as he continues to ram into me. I throw my glance to the side, barely seeing through the curtain of hair in my eyes. My silent watcher is fisting his cock to Jax's drives. Through the window's reflection, Jax's intent face looks down on me. It's a mirror into our past and reminds me how desperate we were that last night together, to ring out every measure of pleasure from our bodies.

But this is different. There's no sweetness. With Jax, and the stranger in the corner office, we are adults satisfying our selfish, erotic urges.

"I want to see your face when you come," he says to my reflection. "I want to see you satisfied."

I'm so close to my release that I bite down my objection. He pulls out of me, turns me around, and pins me to the glass. He kisses me hard, lifting my legs to his hips, he enters me again with rough, urgent thrusts. The cool, slick glass is at my back, contrasting with the heat that radiates off my body. I imagine the show the corner office is getting. Jax's blond hair is plastered to his skull, the wild, hazel eyes looking down on me, his familiar scent marking me as his.

My body trembles as he grinds me. The muscles of his carved arms flex with the effort of keeping me in place and I meet his thrusts, wanting more. We are chest to chest, my release coming. I look into his face, more to see when he's ready. We speak a silent language with our bodies, punctuated by the moan or grunts that escape us until we let go together in a single, beautiful release.

We slide down the length of the glass in a mass, my legs around his waist, his cock sliding free when we reach the carpeted floor. I'm on my back, Jax on top of me at my breast. My breath labored, I perch onto an elbow to look out. I squint, positive it was the same place. There's no chair near the glass. No one watching. The corner office is vacant, a lamp light shining over a desk.

We finish our sexy night in his bed, in one of the guest rooms that's almost as big as the master suite. Sometime after midnight, I slip from the room and return to the master bedroom. It's still a workday, albeit very early. I shower and dress in winter white boots, wool pants, sweater, and a gorgeous camel-color coat. Angela thoughtfully brought me a wool hat, gloves, and scarf to match. I take the rest of my clothes I bought from Angela and the outfit laundered by the hotel in several shopping bags.

Before I leave, I write Jax a note. I scrawl in my less-than-great handwriting: *Wonderful night. Went back to the valley. Our tour begins today. I will meet you at your place.*

I prop the note up on the counter, take a step back, but something catches the heel of my boot. I scoop up the white packet of condoms and slip them into my pocket, call the elevator, and slip past the opening doors. The ambassador on duty calls me a car and I head back to Silicon Valley.

15

Toil and Trouble

My body is working in slow motion on a few hours of sleep, but I would trade a weeks' worth of sleep for another night I had with Jax and a few more. The winding road leading up to his house has the light shine of dew on the asphalt. I think it's best we don't drive his sports car to the locations I've set-up for the district tour. They all know he's wealthy, but he needs to look like a humble public servant. We can take my sedan, if he doesn't have a less conspicuous car in his garage.

My same parking spot is available, but there are a few cars in the circular drive, a couple that weren't here yesterday. One possibly belongs to Bruce, the personal assistant I should have met yesterday. I hope we don't butt heads…better to make him an ally.

A deep tone resonates when I ring the doorbell. I'm looking back at the car park as the door swings open. Brita appears in a familiar flour-dusted apron, annoyed that she has to answer the door again. She looks down at me.

"Ah, Ms. Ivarsson, come." She waves me in. "It is good to see you again. Mr. Jaxson told me you liked my strudel."

My smile prompts one in return with a soft blush over her cheeks.

"It was wonderful," I say, "but I didn't get to finish my portion; we were in a hurry."

Brita's brow shows deep furrows. She folds her arms across her ample chest. "I'll have to make some strudel to go home with you."

My smile turns into a ray of sunshine. I can't believe my luck. "That would be great, thank you."

"Brita? Who's at the door?" A strident voice reaches us from inside the house.

It sounds like Jessica Bennett, calling from the terrace. Why is Jax's mother here? Is she planning to sit in on our meeting? Another more horrifying thought occurs to me that maybe she's coming on the tour.

Jessica escorted around like the king's mother would be a disaster. Then again, it might work to Jax's advantage. His constituents would think he was a wonderful person to have his mother with him. We can work out that angle later.

"Brita." Jessica's calls have reached annoyance. Hard footsteps are approaching.

Brita bites her lip, throwing a panicked glance over her shoulder. Strong fingers dig into my arm. She leans into me with her worried attention. "Gird your loins, girl, the witches are here," she says in a loud whisper. "Gird your loins," she repeats. The pain in my forearm subsides when she releases me to bustle back to her kitchen.

I pass through the foyer into the living room and narrowly avoid knocking Jessica over. She flings a hand up to her throat as I reach out a hand to steady her.

She stares at my offer of help, choosing to ignore it. "I don't know why Brita couldn't tell me you're here. Honestly," she huffs. "She never wants to leave that kitchen. We have to endure a hissy fit any time we ask her to do anything not related to cooking. Never mind, you're here now." She latches onto my arm. "Jaxson is still upstairs. He should be down soon, but I want you to meet his assistant."

She tugs me along at a fast clip across the wide expanse of living room, halting a few feet from the railing. The food table, a sofa, scattered chairs, and the rustic banquet table are ready for breakfast. Even the aromas of fresh-brewed coffee and crispy bacon have me looking forward to a morning meal.

Jessica stands to my side, arms folded, not bothering to make an introduction. My first perception is a high-backed chair turned toward the view. The only clue I have that a person is occupying the seat is crossed legs the length of my body. The gray shoes at the end of those long, slender legs are red-soled high heels.

Jessica pulls me around to face the visitor. An expensive-looking blond regards me in an exquisitely cut pale-gray suit. The wool jacket is folded neatly over the arm of the chair.

"Chloe, I'd like you to meet Jax's assistant, Pamela Bruce."

The woman leans forward, extending a hand, her slender fingers polished with a French manicure.

I change my laptop case to my left hand and clasp her hand.

"Jax told me he had another work spouse," she says, giving me an appraisal. "Welcome to the club. How was the restaurant? He said you two had a meeting in the city."

Jessica's eyebrows raise in a delicate arch. "I didn't hear about a meeting in San Francisco. My son failed to mention anything."

They turn their silent questions toward me. I glance at the living room to see if there will be an assist from my boss. Typical, he's not in sight. I conjure up a plausible explanation anyway. I'll need to go over the story with Jax before he talks with them.

"It was something last minute," I begin the lie. "I put in a call a few days ago to a counterpart in San Francisco. She works for

Councilmember Esper. I asked if they would meet with us to discuss city politics. She called last minute to say they had an unexpected opening in his schedule, and I grabbed the appointment."

Jessica nods her approval like a political advisor. "I don't know that councilmember. In fact, I don't know San Francisco politics, but any insight gained from someone serving a large district could be beneficial to Jaxson."

Pamela shrugs, losing interest in the story. "I'll leave the politicking to you and Chloe. I just need to keep Jaxson on track with his personal schedule. Which reminds me...I need to leave to take care of some errands. I was hoping to see Jaxson before he left for the day." She stands, smoothing her skirt. "I'll give him a call later." Pamela retrieves her jacket and shrugs into it. "It was nice meeting you, Chloe. I'm sure we'll be talking soon to work out Jaxson's schedule." She retrieves her bag and heads toward the living room.

I sink into a chair at the table, watching her exit.

Jessica takes a seat on the sofa and retrieves her coffee cup from a side table. "Pamela has been his assistant since he formed his company. She's a lovely girl."

"Jax says she's very efficient."

"So he did mention her...good."

"Yes, he called her to make reservations at the restaurant yesterday."

I thought Bruce was a male. Jax has that damned habit of calling everyone by their last name. I should have known he wouldn't have a male assistant.

She studies me over the rim of her cup. "I'm glad Jaxson told you about Pamela, and did he also tell you they're engaged?"

A satisfied smile lights her face at my response. I'm pissed that she's seen my surprise. I'd been dismissing Pamela Bruce during our brief meeting, convincing myself that this beautiful, polished woman couldn't be Jax's type. I realize why Jax made that condition last night, that we'd make love only once. I knew deep down there was more to the bargain I was making. I wanted him; why the hell would I look too closely at his offer?

I'm treated to a sigh of pity as Jessica returns her cup to the saucer. "You would have met her at the swearing-in ceremony, but she was with her family on an impromptu vacation that ran longer than expected. It prevented her from coming back in time to celebrate with Jaxson."

I decide coffee is a good idea and walk to the buffet. I'm careful to keep my back to her while I watch Pamela trek through the living room. She stops midway to pull out her phone, pausing to talk.

"That must have been difficult for them," I say, working to regain my composure.

"Those two are such romantics," she coos. "They possibly decided to celebrate when she returned. I grew up with her mother. She comes from an old prominent family. You know, Jaxson met her at Princeton and they dated all through college."

The underlining glee in her voice cuts like a jagged shard of glass pushing through my heart. But it's Brita's advice to gird my loins that forces me to glance at Jessica to let her know I'm not upset with her news.

"You see, Pamela isn't a work spouse. That's someone who gives support, shares in their work partner's job success, but has none of the intimacy." Her gaze drifts to Pamela, who's still on a call. "I'm sure that intimacy might happen to some of those couples, but my son wouldn't cross that line to risk hurting Pamela or his career."

So, she sees my role as his helpmate, but I'll never be in his bed. If I'd heard this information sooner, last night wouldn't have happened. I take inventory. He's engaged, not married. Jax and I were intimate, so that ship has sailed, Jessica. And yeah, your son ran over that line to get to me. I pour brown liquid into my cup. I only have a moment of satisfaction when I realize her deeper meaning. Maybe he would bed me, but I'd never be his wife.

Jax enters the living room as Pamela reaches the end of the space near the stairs. Jax is showered and shaved in dark blue slacks and shirt. He shows no effects from his time with me last night.

He smiles and engages Pamela in conversation. They're a distance away, preventing me from hearing their discussion. She's animated, clearly excited to see him, while Jax nods as he listens. It's hard to watch them together knowing I've lost him. But no, I never had him. She places her hand on his chest, gives him a quick kiss on the cheek and continues toward the foray. Jax watches her leave, his face unreadable.

Jax appears on the terrace with a smile for his mother as he walks over to kiss her cheek. "Good morning, mother," he says. Then he swings his attention to me. "Good morning, Ivarsson. How are you today?"

Was that a glint in his eye?

I'm aware of Jessica's scrutiny. "I'm fine. Are you ready for our tour today?"

"Yes, I'm looking forward to our visits. You'll help me out and answer any questions I have?"

"That's what I'm here for. These initial appointments are in my area of expertise. Next week you'll visit a recycling plant and utilities. Mateo will lead that tour."

"You'll be with us next week, correct?"

"I can be, but it's unnecessary. You'll be a pro by the end of our tour this week. I also think it's a good idea to bond with Mateo without me around."

Jessica clears her throat, rising to her feet. "I'll be leaving now," she announces. "It looks like you're in expert hands with Chloe."

"You're here early, Mother. I thought you were going to join me on the tour."

"I was talking to Pamela yesterday, and she mentioned Chloe

might be here for this meeting. I just wanted to say hello."

Jax studies his mother, but asks nothing. "I'll walk you out," he says, ready to take her arm.

She waves him away. "Why do you insist on escorting me to my car? Do you think I'm incapable of finding my way out?" she teases, happy with her son's attention.

"Mother, I always offer to walk you to your car." He glances at me. "I really want Ivarsson to think I'm a good son," he says in a stage whisper.

"Chloe doesn't need convincing. I'm sure she knows you're an excellent son." She touches his arm to reassure him. "I'm not alone… my driver is here. Brita is feeding him in the kitchen," she sighs. "I have to pry him away from that woman or I'll be late to my Pilates class."

I stand. "It's good to see you, Jessica," I say.

She takes my hand, holding it tight. "Good to see you as well." She places a kiss on my cheek. "Remember what I said, dear," she whispers.

Jax is aware she's said something to me. I look at Jax with an awkward smile.

"Jaxson." She grazes his cheek.

"Mother?"

Jessica Bennett smiles and sweeps off the terrace with a goodbye wave.

I watch Jessica leave while Jax busies himself at the less-copious buffet table. There are only a few items and strudel.

"I was disappointed when I found out you were gone. I was hoping you would have stayed so we could talk," he says, placing his cup beside me, then taking my hand.

"Today's a workday," I say, pulling my hand away. "What kind of a Chief of Staff would I be if I didn't do my job?"

Jax studies me for a moment and understands that I'm not up for a rehash of last night. He wisely decides to take his coffee to the head of the table. "I didn't have the chance to say goodbye to you. I wanted to know if you were alright."

I'm as good as I can be, taking a one-night-only deal from the love of my life. Then, if that wasn't enough, his mother tells me he's engaged.

"I'd rather talk about the district tour." I didn't intend for it to come out as blunt, but it's how I feel. Nothing has changed—I'm still leaving his team—I just need to endure a few more days.

I pull out my laptop and fire it up. I avoid his gaze while rummaging in my bag for papers. "I don't know how you like to receive your information. Here's your agenda." I slide the papers across to him. "There's also a copy in your email.

He moves the papers closer, neatly arranging the three sheets in front of him.

"I scheduled three stops for today. The school district. That will take up a few hours; they'd like you to visit an elementary school. The children have a presentation. A food pantry. This is Peterson's signature project. They want you to see their operation and talk about their outreach efforts. We finish up at Fire Station 38. We'll meet the fire chief and tour the facility."

He glances up from the agenda. "What's expected of me?"

I close my laptop and sit back. "They'll press you to support their programs. Tell them you're still getting your feet wet and that you'll schedule meetings with them to discuss their concerns. Be charming and don't commit. If you get in trouble, I'll be here to help. You can call on me to respond as the policy expert."

"I know you've been busy," he trails off. We both understand what's unsaid. "Have you thought about a platform?"

"I've given it some thought. Energy and the environment are big topics. Pushing a green initiative would help your district and the city."

He thinks about this, then shakes his head. "That's Alcazars' area. I'm not saying it's not important, but I want us to work together."

"Yes, those are Mateo Alcazar's areas, and they're important issues with far-reaching effects that will have an impact on the city even after your tenure."

"I want to know the needs in your areas." He's insistent without being demanding. This is, after all, his show.

I stare out, watching birds take flight. Is he trying to lure me in with a cause that's personal to me, so I won't leave? Did he prostitute himself so I'd stay?

"Public safety, public health, fire, and police. They all have a wide range of concerns like drug use, juvenile delinquency, even littering," I say, turning my attention back to his concerned face.

"You're being evasive. Which of these areas should I concentrate on?" His patience is running thin.

"Police or fire," I shoot back. "Let me know which appeals to you and I'll put something together for you to review."

"Police."

"Done," I say, shoving my laptop back in its case. "We'll need to scramble if we want to make the first stop on time."

We both stand.

"Oh, do you have another vehicle? It's not a good idea to appear in a car that costs much more than the average person makes in a year."

"I've got an SUV, a Toyota Highlander. I use it when I need to do some hauling."

I push away the image of Jax hauling stuff to the dump in a T-shirt and jeans; it's just too average. "That'll work," I say and turn to go, but he catches my hand before I can slip by him. I twist back, but he's holding on.

"This isn't over, Ivarsson. I still want to talk." He pulls me to him, his hand at my back.

I'm waiting for him to say more, so I can cut him off with a protest that we'll be late. But Jax does the unexpected. I get kissed soundly, and I'm melting into the comfort of his firm body. The touch of his lips is all I want. He holds me even tighter, but I can't stop the shouting in my head that he's engaged and a liar by omission. I place my hand on his chest and nudge him away.

He stands there with no words, little expression.

"I promise you'll get your talk, Jax, but you might not like what I have to say."

16

Ring of Fire

*I*t's easy to see why Jax is a rising political star: he's a natural. He's got good instincts and, even more surprising, he takes directions from me without question. But what will serve him well in his public career is something I can't teach him. It's something you can't fake and what few politicians have, which is true empathy for the people they serve.

At the school district and the food pantry, I had to stop him from committing to more than Peterson's legacy. Both programs are worthy of his support, but until he understands his power, and how to use it effectively, it's better to wait.

His choice to build his platform as a law-and-order advocate is not surprising. Peterson was a fierce supporter of the police department. It's likely a secret macho fantasy to be a part of the thin blue line. The police get their share of funding and no department is swimming in money, but the fire department always seems to be the services they cut back.

While we're en route to the fire station, I switch to flat shoes to avoid another spill in that treacherous parking lot. Jax continues to glance down, trying to watch me as I slide off my heels. At one point, I thought he was going to swerve off the road.

"Keep your eyes on the road or you'll kill us both."

He shakes his head and his dimples appear like a mood barometer, meaning that he's amused at my statement, which pisses me off.

There isn't time to talk during our drive between stops. We're too busy with my briefings and me answering his questions to discuss anything personal; it's not the time anyway.

When we arrive at Station 38, Jax knows what to expect. He pulls into the parking lot and kills the engine. I grab for my purse, but he lays his hand on top of mine.

"This is our last stop, Ivarsson. Once we finish here, I want to talk. We can do it in the car, we can wait until I get us back to my house, or we can go somewhere for dinner, but you're not going to put me off any longer."

"We can talk tomorrow," I say as I pull my bag away. "I'm operating on a few hours' sleep and I can't trust myself to have a discussion without nodding off."

He pulls the key out of the ignition and twists his body toward me. "All right, tomorrow then. Can we talk during breakfast?"

"Let's see how it goes." I can't give him any more of an answer than that. It's true I'm operating on fumes and I'll need all my cognitive ability once we talk.

"I don't like how we left this. This happened to both of us. We need to talk this out."

"I agree." Which are the first words I've uttered without an undercurrent of anger since we left his house. He needs to understand that nothing has changed; I'm still leaving his team.

"Are you eager to make a mark on the city?" a muffled voice says from a man whose face is almost pressed against the driver's-side window. I jump at the unexpected figure, then notice there are about ten people behind him.

"Remember what I said about no commitment," I mumble like I'm working a ventriloquist dummy.

Jax nods, releases the door locks, and we slide out. Jax is camera-ready in the midst of a crowd. They thrust microphones in his face, but he handles it like a pro. "To answer your question, I'm just getting my feet wet. I'm here to listen. When we have something to announce, we'll call all of you in for a chat."

They trail behind us like a pack of puppies. Jax stays close to me with a protective hand at my elbow as we walk toward the station. Chief Rehnquist is there to meet us at the entrance. He glowers at the entourage that has stopped a respectful distance away and then greets us.

"Welcome to Fire Station 38. We've been anticipating your visit to our facility since you won your council seat." His gaze falls on me. "Hello, Chloe, it's always good to see you. I heard you were here a few days ago. They said you took a spill in our parking lot and one of the men patched you up. Are you better?"

"Yes, Chief, I'm fine."

"Good, good. You should've told me you planned a visit and I would have met you. Were you here on official business?"

"No, I was dropping off a donation to support your fundraiser."

Jax swings his gaze over to me like he's surprised I'd do anything in the district without his knowledge. I ignore him and concentrate on the flirting chief.

"Well, the fire district thanks you for showing interest in our cause. Please come in." We walk past the chief and the crowd of reporters move en masse to the door.

"You lot stay outside," the chief shouts out to the reporters. "If Councilman Bennett wants to give a statement after our tour, then we'll let you come into the main room."

We tour the station like unseen ghosts observing the crew performing their duties. I trail behind Jax and the chief, watching for Brody's imposing form or his friendly face. What do I call someone who appears when I need saving? I can tell you it raises expectations that Brody's protection will arrive after any rough patch with Jax, and today got pretty bumpy. I tune back into the chief's tour and tell myself Brody's not working today or he hasn't arrived for his shift.

We round the corner and the chief pauses at the photos on the memorial wall of fallen firefighters. This part always pulls at my heart, that these men died protecting the community, leaving people they loved behind. He praises their sacrifice and reminds us the present crew have the same courage and commitment to their work.

We move on in a somber mood that isn't lightened by viewing some dilapidated parts of the facility, built in the '80s.

We're edging along the wall of a large, sad, windowless dormitory. It's not quite out of a Dickens story, but it's close.

"Our living quarters are too old and cramped for a modern-day fire station. The city talks about renovating this place, but if I have a say, they should build a brand-new facility. Let's move into the apparatus bay to see the engines."

We step through a dim passage toward the vast apparatus bay that houses three gleaming fire trucks. The crew is mysteriously absent from the area; our footsteps echo as we move around the machinery.

The chief stops us in front of the largest truck and pats the front of the most impressive fire engine. "We also propose that Station 38 be a training facility. The lot in the back, you can see it from here," he gestures to the open bay doors, "isn't owned by the city. Two years ago, we were all set to buy that property. That was the last year of the drought. It took a lot more of our resources and money, and now we're not sure when we can move forward. I know your predecessor wasn't big on championing the fire department. His interests lie with the police, which is a good cause, but the community needs this fire station and training facility to keep up to date. Can I count on your support?"

I give Jax an imperceptible *don't commit* look, but he's avoiding my gaze.

"I mean, you see the need," Chief Rehnquist continues, "and you live in District 5. What if it was your house that was on fire?"

Jax takes in the place's enormity, fire engines and equipment at the ready. I try to give him another *don't commit* signal, but he won't look at me.

"I understand, Chief Rehnquist. I'm on a listening tour and my office will arrange for a time we can sit and speak more about your concerns."

I let out my breath, relieved that my advice has finally penetrated.

We find ourselves back in the main room and the reporters come to attention when they see us enter. There's glass between us, but it doesn't stop them from shouting questions. Jax looks at me with a what do we do now? look.

I pull on his sleeve. "You should talk to them. Give them a brief, noncommittal statement and answer a few questions. If you get stuck, introduce me as your policy expert." He nods like we've been doing this forever. Even now, looking at him, I get a brief flutter in my stomach. Too many feelings rise up at odd times. Is this what love feels like or is this lust? He gives me a private smile, then pushes through the door to the waiting reporters.

"We don't have much time, but I can take a few questions," Jax announces to the waiting crowd.

"How was your tour, Councilman Bennett?" a woman says with a sly smile.

"Hello, Katie, good to see you." Jax acknowledges her with a grin. "Have you changed from writing tech pieces to writing political articles?"

"No," she quips back like she knows him, "I'm assigned to cover you no matter what you're up to."

There's a titter of laughter running through the crowd, but I don't find it funny. Could he know her intimately? She looks ready to lick her lips like he's a gigantic piece of chocolate cake. I shake the thought away. This won't be my problem; I'm leaving at the end of the week.

"Chief Rehnquist gave us an insightful tour. I'm glad we had some time to talk."

"Will you follow in the footsteps of your predecessor and ignore the needs of the fire department?" A young male reporter calls out.

I recognize him. He's been covering politics for San Pacitas for a couple of years. He's known for fiery commentary, has had some lead stories in the *San Pacitas News*, and is becoming a political force himself.

"I'll schedule time with the chief to discuss his concerns," Jax replies.

"So, what you're saying is that it will be the status quo in District 5 and the police will get the lion's share of monies."

"I don't think that's fair to say at this stage."

"You ran on more access to services and the people of District 5 having more say in government. Polls have shown that this is a needed project that has overwhelming support by the people of this district and the city."

"I made those promises before the election, and I stand by my platform."

"Then will you make a promise now, to lobby for the fire department's renovation of Fire Station 38 and build the proposed training facility?"

There's silence, the kind of silence that marks a defining moment. Jax glances at me, but we haven't coordinated enough for me to give him a signal that he would understand. He should continue to restate his noncommittal stance at this point and not fall into the reporter's trap, or he risks sounding like another politician. This isn't a good start for a councilmember who was elected to be a change agent. I catch movement out of the corner of my vision. Members of the fire station crew form a loose group behind the press, men and women waiting for an answer. Maybe a savior. Brody is there, a head taller than everyone else and dressed in his uniform. He must have stayed out of our way while we toured, or he just got here for his shift. We make a connection when he catches my gaze.

His attention rattles me, and I step closer to Jax as if making it clear who I'm with. I'm about to pull Jax's sleeve to whisper that he should introduce me when he raises a hand in an *I've got this* gesture without looking at me. I'm a little proud and a bit frightened that he's taking control.

"No, I won't continue the status quo. My campaign stood for change, and I'll make a promise to start now to find the funds the fire department has requested. You'll need to give us, my staff and I, time to coordinate with the fire department, but after, we'll make a join announcement."

The unexpected commitment stuns the crowd. Brody looks at me as if to say, *Is this guy for real?* I just look up at Jax with my professional, *I'm with the greatest politician in the world* look plastered on my face and hope he's serious. The press coverage will be good today; they'll broadcast his promise. Later they'll hold him to his commitment and will examine his every decision for the project until it's done, then grumble how it could have been done better. I was hoping for more time to cement his political direction, but he just ended his honeymoon period.

"Sorry to cut this short, but we have another appointment," he says, regaining the momentum. "I'll see you all when we call a press conference on this matter. Have a great evening."

Jax eases the SUV into heavy traffic. We're stopped at a light when he looks over at me with a sheepish grin. "Looks like I put my foot in it. I guess I don't have to tell you to scrap the suggestions for the police department and concentrate on Fire Station 38."

I find my heels near my feet and cross my legs to change out of my flats.

He glances down. "Damn, Ivarsson, you're distracting when I'm trying to have a conversation. Do you have to show that much thigh?"

"Keep your eyes on the road and you won't have that problem." The bandage on my knee is loose, so I hike my foot on the edge of the seat to reposition it to lie flat.

"I guess I should be grateful you're not eating an ice cream," he grumbles.

I can't help it; I laugh, and he joins me. That chuckle gives us a surge of energy to pitch suggestions for the Station 38 funding—some interesting, some wildly unusable—until my tired brain hits a wall. We lapse into silence, waiting for traffic lights to change, comfortable with our own thoughts.

Jax pulls his car next to my little sedan. His house is a soft yellow glow against the backdrop of the dark-blue evening. It's inviting, like there's someone waiting for him inside and when he's settles in, they'll share a meal and talk about their day. No cars in the driveway. I assume the house is empty, but I could be wrong.

I open my door, breathing in the dark, crisp January evening. It's not my favorite time of year; I'm the happiest when the clocks switch forward and there's more light in my day. I slam the door, hoisting my bags on my shoulder, and walk towards my car. Jax stands just outside the parking lot lights, not quite a shadowy figure.

"Thanks for your help, Ivarsson, I couldn't have survived without you by my side. It felt natural. I thought we made a great team."

He's not wrong. The synergy was there today. Everything went as planned until the end, and even Peterson wouldn't have handled it better. I open my door and pitch the bags inside. "You're a natural," I say. "You have the makings of a great politician, one who's in it for the right reasons and actually cares about the people he serves."

He hesitates for a few moments. I know he's taking in the praise; I imagine him preening like a lion.

"Can I interest you in a coffee?" he says. "My latte machine is better than the Max's and I can be your personal barista."

I lean against the car, arms folded, gazing up into the sky. You can see the stars from here with no other homes around, and there's the view of the lights flickering in the valley below.

"It's funny how we have these dreams, but when they come to life, the reality is never quite how we imagine."

"Last night," he says, settling next to me. "It wasn't what you expected?"

We're two people looking up at the sky, trying to muster the words we should say.

"If you're talking about the night we spent together, I enjoyed our time. I'm feeling philosophical…a long day does that to me." I push away from the car. "Thanks for the offer of coffee, but I should go. We have a lot of work in front of us."

"I'd like you to stay, Ivarsson, I think you need to."

That garners a look from me.

"If you're too tired to drive, stay the night. I've got plenty of room."

His house looks cozy, but is this concern for my well-being? "What, and endanger your one-night-only stipulation?" I toss it out as a jab, wondering if he'll take the bait.

"Maybe it's inappropriate, but I'd feel responsible if anything happened to you. I'm not saying this as part of my campaign to convince you to stay on my team." His voice has a throaty murmur. "You staying here, that can be anything you want it to be."

He's close, inches close.

"Let's have a do-over," he says. "The Max didn't count. You deserve more than us making love in a hotel room. Stay with me tonight." His movements are fluid in the diffused light. I don't register his finger until it has gently traced the length of my jaw. How can his face be so clear in the dark? Can I really see the hazel of his eyes?

"What do you say?"

I don't answer. How many do-overs would he allow until he's walking down the aisle with Pamela and I'm just a mistress? His finger drifts to the hollow of my throat. A wave of want fills me, and it nearly pushes me to the ground. I drop my arms, pressing my hands flat against the car. God, I want to be warm in his bed with his hard body wrapped around mine.

I stop the sensory memory, the wanting him. He's engaged. I know this now and I can't feign ignorance, even if he's not willing to honor his commitment. How will he explain me in the same clothes when his fiancée arrives in the morning?

He pulls me to him. My head and hands rest on his chest. I breathe him in, enjoying these moments, but it's short-lived. I decide I can't do this. I make sure he can see my face. "Thanks for the offer, but I'm leaving." My hoarse whisper gives too much away.

I get a kiss in reply, a passionate one that has me shaking with his intensity. I stir, regretting what comes next. I won't do it; I can't be that desperate for him to want me. "No," I say in a small voice.

It's enough for his hands to fall away. Jaxson Bennett isn't used to the word no. He accepts my rejection, steps back, and turns away, wiping my lipstick off with the back of his hand. "I'll see you tomorrow then?"

I open the door. Regret for what I've done deepens the hurt. I slide into the driver's side anyway, white-knuckle the steering wheel, and exhale a ragged breath. "Yes, tomorrow."

17

Stand In

A light shines in the living room of the dark house. Kurt slumps in an oversized recliner asleep with a laptop balanced dangerously on his lap and a car crashing in a German action movie, set at an ear-splitting volume. He wakes with a start as I step inside the room.

"Schatz?" he says, trying to focus his blurry vision on me. If he were awake, he'd know I wasn't his wife. My sister Kellis is almost a foot taller than me.

"Hi, Kurt, it's me, Chloe," I shout over the gunfire.

"Ah, Chloe. What time is it?" he says, using the heel of his hands to wipe the sleep from his eyes. "I was working and watching a good movie."

I pick up the remote from the coffee table and hit pause to preserve my hearing. Beautiful silence descends.

"Hey." His protest is halfhearted. "I was watching that."

"It's difficult to watch a movie with your eyes closed…where's

Kellis?"

I find a music station, some coffeehouse soft rock he likes. "It's about 11:30. I had a couple of appointments after work, then went for a drive. I guess the time got away from me."

A huge yawn prevents him from speaking. He stops and raises his arms over his head for a catlike stretch. "Schatz was tired. I told her to go to bed."

Unease tightens my stomach, reminding me I should have at least texted her this evening. I glance at the hall...maybe I should check on her. "Is it the baby?"

"Yeah, it's partly the baby, managing her company, and a little bit worrying about you. She was concerned when you didn't come home last night, even after you sent her a text."

I chew my lip, feeling guilty I wasn't here. Kellis needed me, and I'm making her worry.

"No, don't do that. You're not a bad sister. She's pregnant. She's going to have good days and bad days. It isn't realistic for you to quit your job and stay by her side every minute. I suggested she go to bed and offered to wait up for you."

"You're a good brother-in-law," I chide.

"Yes, and don't you forget it."

"What did you guys have for dinner?" I say, heading for the kitchen. There have got to be leftovers. "You can keep me company while I microwave something."

"Why don't you get comfortable and I'll get your dinner. You look like you need to talk. I'm not Kellis, but I can listen."

See, that's why I love this guy and thought he was perfect for my sister. "Deal. I'll shower, change, and be right back."

I return to the kitchen as Kurt is about to finish placing everything on a tray.

"You need to relax. Have your dinner in the living room." He lifts the tray and I almost skip to the next room, happy to be looked after. I sink into the overstuffed couch while he sets the tray on the coffee table, unfurls the couch blanket, and places it on my lap. I don't remember ever being spoiled like this. I take that back. When I was sick, Mom brought me soup.

"I had schnitzel delivered from Naschmarkt and they sent this Austrian wine along with the meal," he says, pouring a glass for me and one for himself. He returns to the recliner, balancing his glass on the armrest. I stab my fork into a breaded piece of pork and savor a mouthful. "This is so good, thank you."

"Someone has to make sure you two are eating well, or we'd be eating pizza and toaster pastry every day. I'm lucky there's a restaurant that will cook German food."

"I thought you said this was an Austrian restaurant?"

"Yes, that cooks good German food. Tell me what happened last night."

I take a sip of my wine and sit back. Whatever I would have confided in Kellis, she would have shared with her husband. I trust Kurt, I always have, so that's not an issue. I set the glass down. I reveal the whole story, but even I think it sounds like a Latin telenovela. Kurt listens without reaction or comment. When I finish, I retrieve the plate and take a bite because I'm still starving. I point my fork at him. "What do you think?"

"I think it's difficult to overrule the heart."

"I'll put that on a T-shirt. What's Jax doing?"

"I was talking about Jaxson. He's conflicted. Engaged to one woman, intense attraction to another. I'm betting he thought his one night with you would satisfy his lust, and then he could walk away after. Think of it as scratching an itch. He hadn't counted on it blowing up in his face."

"Are you saying I have a chance with him?"

Kurt raises an eyebrow. "You have a good chance, but do you want to break up an engagement?"

I trade my plate for the wine glass, sink back into the couch, and hold my glass with two hands. "No, I don't want to be that woman," I say with a sigh. I drink deeply, seeing myself as a red-lipped, tight-dressed, slut tempting him away from Pamela and me living my HEA with Jax.

I shake my head. I can't believe I'm considering such a bitch move. My attraction for Jax is making me cross lines. How can I justify that, even if I could get him back?

"Do you want my advice?"

He breaks into my disturbing thoughts before they can go into freefall. "I'd like your take on this troubling mess. I'm counting on you and Kellis to be my clear-eyed barometers."

"You've been proactive with the coordinator, requesting to leave his staff. The cooling-off period she suggested is almost over. When the time comes, tell her you haven't changed your mind and move on."

"What about the fire department?" I think about Brody and the other firefighters at the station that hope Jax's promise might be real.

"You still have a little time. Find a solution and let someone else run with it. You're leaving behind a capable staff, right?"

"Yes, but no one has the fire department expertise. I mean, not as extensive as my knowledge."

"I'm sure there's someone up and coming who would jump at the chance to work with Councilman Bennett. It might be a career-defining opportunity."

He's right...it's the kind of opportunity that could get me into the City Manager's office. I've been so focused on my feelings, I didn't think about my position in those terms. Could I take the battering to my heart and still do my job?

"Chloe, I didn't want to say this in front of Kellis, but now that it's just the two of us... I'm concerned."

My brother-in-law is not the chatty type. If he's concerned, it's got to be serious. "What is it? Is this about my sister?"

"No," he says quickly, but he's still having trouble framing what he wants to say. "Nothing about Kellis. I know she's concerned too, although she's never said, but it must be on her mind. All the time I've known you, there's been no one serious in your life until this Jaxson. I don't think you should place all your hopes in one man until you're sure."

The observation has me sitting up and drawing my knees to my chest. This must be what it's like to have an older brother. "I date, but I just haven't found anyone special enough to meet my family. No one that makes my temperature rise," I tease, then Brody's bad-boy grin from the firefighter's calendar comes to mind. A man who has sexy coming off of him in waves. We've met a few times when he's rescued me, but Brody hasn't attempted to get to know me.

"I think I can help. Remember when you considered that ridiculous plan to make Jaxson jealous?"

"I remember."

"Give me a minute. Let me just grab something from the office." When he returns, he hands me a large folder before he sits down. "We talked about the possibilities of a German man posing as your boyfriend."

I nod and glance down at the folder in my hand.

"Ana sent me some prospects yesterday and I've reviewed them online, but I also asked her to send me hard copies of photographs and resumes. You're holding the results."

I open the folder.

"You may not need a fake boyfriend, but this might be a solution to finding a genuine relationship. Wouldn't it be great if all four of us could live in Munich together? Your parents and siblings would always be welcome." I get the vision of all four of us living in a house together like in a sitcom. I bite back a funny response when I remember his parents practically abandoned him when he was a kid. Family is everything to him. I'm happy he thinks I'm a part of his family.

Kurt finds his laptop and scrolls through information. "The first candidate is Günter. He's 26 and has an engineering degree. We're grooming him for upper management. He likes nature, cycling, football. He is quite a big man, about 6'3" and fit. What do you think?"

I pull out an 8 x 10 color photo of a very serious man in a suit. He's good looking, but he looks very similar to Kurt in face and build.

"I know you shouldn't be reviewing this with your brother-in-law. Why don't you take the photos and information and study them in private? I've gone over the original batch of candidates and thought these were the best of the lot. If you like any of them, I'll have them flown out here to meet you, or you can get the ball rolling and do a little FaceTime. At least you'll know who you really want to see."

"Thank you, Kurt. This was thoughtful. I'll look over these photos and tell you what I think."

He gets up, stretching a bit, satisfied that he's solved my problems. "I'm glad we had this talk. You're a good person; you need a man who's worthy of your love. I hope this works out." He scoops up his laptop and strides out of the room. Before reaching the hallway, he hesitates. "I almost forgot. Kellis would be angry with me if I had forgotten to give you this message. Your mother called and gave your sister a foretelling for you. She's written it down. It's that blue envelope on the coffee table. Good night."

I don't know what's scarier, Kurt clones or my mom's prediction. I pick up the envelope and slide a finger under the flap. I pull out the heavy paper and unfold it, laying it out on the table. The simple, but perplexing, message is written in my mother's neat cursive handwriting.

When sweet love brings a life from pain, true nature never changes.

18

Quorum

*P*amela stands in the doorway, greeting me with a gracious smile. I see why Jax loves her…she's bright, easy, and exudes old money. They would cast her as the wife of a prominent politician if she didn't already have the job.

I rock a solid middle-class vibe with my off-the-rack suit. That patina of wealth could have been mine if they had raised me with money from the beginning.

Pamela's presence reminds me that I wouldn't be in this mansion if I didn't work for Jax. I smile and enter the foyer, knowing I'm an intruder. There's awkwardness from me, imagining her relationship with Jax and that she's had him all these years after our break-up. She tosses her head back with a small laugh, talking about her drive over here. It proves my short past with Jax doesn't affect her. Why would it? She's had the luxury of time building a bond with him. I glance down the long hallway for Brita, willing her to rescue me from these feelings that won't go away, and, unlucky me, there's no sign of the flour-coated baker.

"If you're looking for the cook, she refused to leave her kitchen today. The rest are on the terrace."

I'm someone who cares about punctuality. Even arriving a few minutes late puts me in a mood. I pull back the sleeve from my wrist to check how late I've arrived.

"Don't worry, we've only been here for about ten minutes. We're early and Jaxson lives here. You're right on time. But you'd better hurry if you want the last of the strudel." She slips her arm under mine and we walk across the living room like two old friends from school. "What's going on with Jaxson? Is it something I should know about?" she says.

The question appears to be a simple concern, but something is warning caution. I wasn't with Jax last night. I can't be blamed for disturbing his rest. Maybe this is just casual conversation?

"He was fine after our press conference, but it's not unusual to have doubts. The decision to support the fire department is an enormous project for a first-term councilmember to take on."

She slows her long strides just before we reach the terrace and releases me. "You're probably right. He's filled us in on the district tour and the press conference at the fire station. I suppose it's the duties of a councilmember, but I've never seen him this worried."

That's something new, Jax worried about something. We enter the terrace and conversation between Jessica and Jax stops.

"Good morning, Chloe." The greeting is borderline curt from Jessica.

Jax and Pamela glance at each other.

"Good morning, Jessica. I hope you're well today."

Jessica pulls the halves of her cardigan tighter around her slim frame. "I'm well," she huffs, looking up at her son, "but I could be better."

I smile and nod at the upset Jessica, while Jax shoots daggers at his mother.

"Pamela promised that I would have the last of the strudel," I say, moving to the buffet. The generous portion is hiding underneath a silver dome. I'd much rather march through the house and back to my car after that greeting from Jessica, but Jax is saying sorry with his eyes. Pamela was right; Jax looks haggard.

"Would you like me to pour your coffee?" Jax offers.

"Stop hovering, Jaxson," Jessica snaps. "Let the girl get her own food. You don't need to wait on her."

A thought tugs at me that whatever they were discussing before I arrived must've had something to do with me.

"If she needs someone to wait on her, we can get Brita out here. Isn't that what you pay her for?"

"Mother…" It sounds like a respectful warning. "I was displaying thoughtfulness to my guest. The way you taught me." Jax glances at me. "If you'd like a latte, I'll ask Britta to make you one."

"I'm fine." I pour my coffee and dump in cream. I take my place at the long, sleek wood table. The low floral arrangement of winter greenery is beautiful after the holidays. I'm as far away as I can get from the snapping Jessica on the couch, but I'm staring across at perfect Pamela. I decide that's my name for her, but then decide against it. I can't be catty to someone this nice; it would be like kicking a kitten.

"I think it's a good idea to start the meeting," Jax announces. We all nod an agreement. "Thank you for coming so early. I've already briefed you on my tour, and what I thought we could do now is to have a brainstorming session."

Pamela speaks up. "So, you're trying to think of ways to help fund the new fire station and training facility? I know little about how city government works, but do you introduce a bill and try to get the other members to agree?"

Jax looks over at me. I take that as my cue to make the explanation. "This year's budget has already been approved and, unless there is an emergency, the funds that were allocated for the fire department this year are all that they'll receive. I think what Jax is looking for is another revenue stream."

"That's right. Well said, Ivarsson. I've asked you to come because you've both been involved with fundraising."

"I see them out on the street all the time in their uniforms getting donations from the cars. Has that brought in any money?" Pamela asks.

"That brings in some, but nothing close to what they'll need," Jax replies.

Jessica clears her throat. "When my charities need money, we run events like an art and wine auction."

Jax glances at me. "What do you think about having a society function?"

"I think you should aim bigger. I—"

"Well, if you don't like that idea," Jessica cuts me off. "We could have a Monte Carlo night."

I stare her down. She's treating me like a servant. Better to assert myself. "It would be good to attract people from society, but to get the money we need, we should appeal to companies. We're fortunate that several multinational companies make their headquarters here in Silicon Valley."

Deep furrows etch Jessica's face; she's digging in for a battle. "I don't see the difference. These are all people with money."

"The fire department needs more than a couple of million dollars," Jax adds.

Jessica is about to respond, but I direct my comment to her. "You need to think about branding, how taking part in a fundraiser for the fire department will benefit their companies and cement them as part of the community. We should also get an ongoing commitment from each company, not just one donation."

"We could have a fundraising concert," Pamela offers. "Maybe we can get some famous people to donate a performance for the cause."

If we're going to pitch useless ideas for an hour, I need to get out of here. Then something occurs to me. It's so blindingly brilliant, it would be a natural. "How about upgrading a fire department tradition?" I say, silencing my audience. "Why don't we throw a Fireman's Ball?"

"I think I might know someone famous to perform at a concert," Pamela says, ignoring my suggestion.

"Who?" says Jax.

"Some old rocker my dad knows. He doesn't play much, but I bet my dad could get him out of retirement. He played with a band named after an animal, or was it a bug?"

They go on like I haven't spoken. Jax names bands from the '80s and Pamela continues to parrot "I don't remember" to every suggestion, while Jessica rolls her eyes. Now I'm officially in hell. I'm planning an escape to the bathroom just to have a break from this madness. Why would Jax think this was a good idea?

"I have an idea," Jessica says. That strong utterance is enough to stop the guess-who questions.

Jax turns an expectant look to his mother. She adjusts her cardigan, enjoying the attention. I turn my body to get the full effect of this monumental idea. It's probably something tired like a costume gala where we all have to come as Alice in Wonderland characters. Jessica could be the Queen of Hearts screaming, "Off with their heads."

"Don't keep us in suspense," Jax prods. "I've only scheduled an hour for this meeting, then Chloe and I have to head for the office."

"Don't rush me, Jaxson. This is so delicious I don't know why I didn't think of it earlier."

"Come on, Jessica, tell us," Pamela whines, "I bet it's brilliant."

She gives us a catbird smile. "Alright, and I think you're going to love it. Why don't we have a Fireman's Ball?" She says this while

157

opening her arms wide like she's imparting a gift.

There's silence for a few seconds while I hear screams going off in my head.

"You know, it might work," Jax says. "Ivarsson, what do you think? Will companies get on board with something like this?"

Three pairs of excited eyes are waiting for me to give the final thumbs-up. Maybe I didn't say my suggestion out loud or I've just crossed into a strange alternate universe. Jessica's smug face is almost too much to stand. "I think it's the perfect idea," I say.

The two give a cheer. Pamela even does a few claps of appreciation. I'm done with this craziness; I'm leaving.

"Mother, now that you came up with this great idea, let's get down to the granular level and start planning. What do you think of—?"

She cuts him off before he can finish his thought. "Dear, you always know I'm the idea person. Once I've established the theme, I let others run with it. I've done my job. It's time for me to get my driver and leave or I'll be late for my aquatic aerobics class."

"Mother, you know it would be helpful if you'd stay."

"I can always give the final approval once the major outline is done. I can tell you then if you're going in the right direction." She pushes away from the couch. "Let me know when you're further along in the planning and I'll attend another meeting."

She looks at Jax. "Don't bother to walk me out. I'll pick up my driver from the clutches of Brita on the way out. Have a good meeting."

I'm stunned as we all watch the woman leave the terrace. When she slips into the foyer, I throw a look at Jax.

"Would you like some more coffee, Ivarsson?" he says.

"Sure, I mean, thank you." That's as much as I can stutter out as he moves to the buffet. Pamela leans forward. I'm surprised that she's capable of a cunning smile. "Good job on the suggestion of the Fireman's Ball."

I search her face for the joke. "You heard me?"

Jax sets a cup in front of me. "Hell, yeah, we heard you, and so did Mother. We hoped that if we ignored you, she might just pick up on your suggestion. She's done it before and she did it again."

"Okay, I give up. Why the ruse?"

"Sorry, Bruce, did you want some coffee as well?" Jax asks.

"No, I'm good." She looks over at me. "Because she's been going on about her planning a fundraiser for the fire department since Jaxson's press conference on the news. I had to invite Jessica to this meeting. Once we agreed on a theme, she would disappear, leaving us to work without any concern until she attends the ball. We didn't have time to fill you in; we thought this would be settled before you arrived."

"How did you know she would take my idea?"

"We didn't," Jax says. "We decided to push the concert idea, but then you came up with the Fireman's Ball. We knew if we ignored you, she would snap up the suggestion."

"If this was all a ruse to prevent her from meddling in the fundraiser, then why was she angry when I walked in? It had to be about me; you stopped talking when I arrived."

Jax glances at Pamela. Something passes between them that I can't read. Jax brings his gaze to me. "My mother was just upset that a party had to be cancelled. It had nothing to do with you. She was angry with me."

"I don't know if you realize this yet," says Pamela, "but Jessica feels threatened by you. When that happens, she overcompensates."

I didn't think anything could threaten Jessica; it's more likely they're both lying.

Jax glances at his watch. "I'm scheduled to tour the new recycling plant with Alcazar today. Bruce and I have a few things to discuss about my personal schedule. We'll talk when I get back into the office. Thanks for helping me out today."

.

19

Let it Linger

There are actual notes piled on my desk, and the call light on my phone looks like a cherry on top of a cop car during a high-speed pursuit. I sink into my seat, wondering how I feel about leaving Jax with his fiancée. That's easy: betrayed and used.

Today I'll talk with Jax and make it clear nothing will stop me from leaving his team. This will finally end our stupid game of *will you won't you* we're playing. I don't care what earth-shaking opportunity he offers working with him; I want out. One week in this job has to be enough to convince Arlene that I've given it a fair chance to work.

My chair squeaks as I move it from side to side, examining the other problem. I've been avoiding thinking about how I've made this situation with Jax worse, but my one night with him wasn't enough for closure. I realize I want him more, and this still isn't settled.

Light tapping on my door distracts me from my self-pity for a moment, then a head pops in, sporting a shy smile. "Good morning,

Chloe," says a cheerful Samir.

It's interesting that he's using my first name. "Good morning. What brings you to my office, or did you stop by because you just wanted to say hi to me?"

Surprise widens his eyes, and he's speechless for a moment. I shouldn't tease him, but he's a cute kid and it's refreshing to talk to a sweet, uncomplicated male.

"I always want to say hi to you," he says, stumbling over the words like he's admitting his attraction, "but Mayor Monica sent me over. She'd like to see you in her office as soon as possible."

Before I knock, a "come in" issues from behind the mayor's door that's opened a crack.

"Good morning, Mayor. Did you want to see me?"

Monica takes off her oversized reading glasses to glance up at me. "Yes, I did. How are you, Chloe?"

I sigh, hoping that's not a loaded question. She nods at me to take a seat.

"Personally, I'm fine."

She turns in her chair. "I suppose I should ask about your working life?"

It seems my request has come to the mayor's ears. I'm not surprised that Arlene and the mayor would talk; Jax is a high-profile councilmember.

"My working life could be better."

"I see. Arlene has told me you requested a transfer to another team. She said you cited differences. Is this true?"

"Our working styles are too different to work together."

"She said you also asked about the Assistant City Manager's position?"

"I did. Then you must know I'm interested. I want to be considered when you open the job."

I think you'd be an excellent Assistant City Manager, but that position won't be available for some time. That opening will post next year."

"There's another reason I'd like to work on a new team. I want to work with a section of the city that has more economic challenges with a more diverse population."

Monica steeples her fingers, choosing her words. "You don't come from that area, yet you want the experience. You've always been a perceptive analyst. The work you did for Councilman Peterson was exceptional. I was hoping you would do the same for Councilman Bennett."

"Thank you for the compliment, but our differences are real, and they would be difficult to overcome."

She swivels her chair to study her view of downtown. "You know, Chloe, I've known Jaxson for a long time. I was one of his supporters who convinced him to run for that council seat. He can be unconventional, but I think he's what District 5 and the city need."

I'd forgotten Monica and Jax were in the same political party. His success would be important to her.

"I'm sorry, but there are a number of analysts that can help him. Why does it need to be me?"

"I've spoken to Jaxson, and he has nothing but praise for you. I don't see why we can't work something out." She returns her attention to me to press the request.

We're at an impasse. I like Monica she's been great to work with, but I just can't continue to work with Jax and keep my sanity. "I would like the transfer."

Monica gives a resigned sigh. "I see this is going to take more than a personal plea from me to convince you to stay."

Saying no could make it difficult for me at the city, but not impossible. At least it would be work hell, and I can handle that.

"I've reviewed your personnel file and you have more than enough experience and education for the assistant's position. Next year when that job posts, I promise I will take your application seriously."

That's a weak offer. She must think I'm an intern wanting my first job. "If you want to bargain, I want the Assistant City Manager position."

She feigns a convincing surprise. "I can't just promise you the job. I'll need to post it, accept applications, do interviews."

I'm almost in awe. This is what it's like to experience Monica's legendary negotiating skills, but she forgets I've seen her in action with the council all these years.

I sit back, not impressed with the offer. "Do whatever needs to be done. In the end, it's still an appointment by the mayor with a confirmation from the council, which you control. You can choose whoever you want to fill that job. I'll need it in writing, before I agree to stay."

"Will you stay his entire term?"

"I'll stay until I start the Assistant City Manager's position."

"What we're agreeing to is your full support of Councilman Bennett. You'll keep him on course and curb any wild impulses that will reflect badly on his term. His time on the council should be a learning experience, but also the foundation of his political career. To be blunt, don't let him screw it up."

"Agreed. When will I receive the letter?"

"Today. Let Jaxson know as soon as possible that you'll stay on his team."

I'm finishing up emails when my cell comes to life. The face of Councilman Bennett flashes across the screen. I answer.

"Ivarsson, I just got back to my office. The recycling tour with Alcazar was fantastic. It was an excellent suggestion that I work with him alone. I'm not saying we had a bromance, but I think we're on the same page."

I change the phone to my other ear. "I'm glad it worked out with Mateo...I mean, Alcazar. I still can't get used to you using our last names.

A chuckle comes through from his end.

I ignore him. "No tour tomorrow. We need to prepare for your first council meeting."

"Yeah, I saw that on the agenda... It's about 3:30 and I'm starving. I'd like to take you to lunch. Somewhere local and we can talk about the Fireman's Ball. And Ivarsson, don't say you've already eaten. You can watch me. I'm leaving for your office now."

The lunch crowd has disappeared from the popular Pruneyard Plaza. When we arrive at Luna, we're given our pick of tables.

We discuss the new influx of restaurants in the city until the server slips a plate in front of Jax. He eats while I nibble on the occasional tortilla chips until I push them away. We talk about his tour and I answer questions about the upcoming council meeting.

"How are we approaching this Fireman's Ball?" he says.

"I've been thinking. It's an old term and isn't politically correct. What do you think of the Firefighter's Ball?"

"I like that. Anything with fighter in it sounds cocky." He's flirting. Was that Mateo or Pamela that's got him in this mood? I'd say it's Mateo; he's a closet comedian with his running commentaries when we're working together.

"I'll put the Firefighter's Ball down as the proposed name for the event."

"Seriously, what's our plan for the ball?"

"I know someone who specializes in these events. He can take the lead with the logistics. I would suggest forming a committee with the fire department or with whoever is in charge of their fundraising."

He steals a chip from the basket, dipping it in the hot salsa.

"When can we meet with the chief?"

"Soon. We need to create a presentation and secure financial commitments after planning to offset the initial costs."

He sits back, throwing his napkin on the table. "My old company will support the event, but I thought all we needed to do was to find a few companies to throw in some money and have a party."

I refuse the chip basket he pushes toward me. "That's what most people think. There's a lot more planning before we get to the fun stuff. It would be great if you'd make a personal plea to your CEO buddies."

"I've got an idea," he says, like it's a sign from above. "Why don't we have a cocktail party, invite all the heavy hitters, and I'll pitch funding the fire department project, maybe create a little competition."

"I don't see a problem. We should run the initial idea by the chief to get his buy-in and confirm there's no conflict with a Firefighter's Ball. If there's interest, we'll do some preliminary work, then meet with the fire department."

"Great, it looks like you've got this under control." The chair legs scrape the floor as he pushes away from the table. "Why don't we walk around the plaza and talk? I haven't seen the Pruneyard since they added those new restaurants."

We stroll out to the plaza, skirting the blue gorilla sculptures and the children's play area.

"I've got to get this out of the way. Have you decided if you're staying on the team?"

He's hopeful, and I don't doubt Monica will do what she promised, but it isn't a done deal until I have my letter in hand.

It's sad that I have to admit defeat. Whatever was growing between us, it will never become a relationship. I need to accept Pamela and their eventual marriage, which I'll probably have to witness since I'm his Chief of Staff.

Jax is holding his breath, waiting for the verdict. It's too soon to commit to staying on his team. "I promised not to make my decision until Friday. I'll give you my answer then. I thought you were going to use every second to convince me?"

His mouth quirks up at my attempt to lighten the mood. "I guess that will have to do for now. Let's discuss more of the personal concerns."

We continue through a side alley lined with shops. Jax walks close alongside me as I check artfully arranged window displays. To others, we must seem like a regular couple spending time together.

A shoe display catches my eye. I stop to admire several pairs of red high heels. Jax hovers. Out of the corner of my vision, he appears uncertain how to begin the conversation about our night at the Maxwell.

Jax leans against the window, vying for my attention. "I feel I've handled us wrong from the start. Since we met, I've been acting like the corporate me, that annoying guy that analyzes, sets goals, and goes after what he wants. I know the player reputation the press like to promote, but that's never been me."

I take some responsibility for where we are now. I encouraged him, but I thought I was making my feelings known to a man free of commitments. Kurt was right—Jax needed to scratch, and that itch was for me. I note the tightrope he's walking, trying to make his case, but I know what's coming. He'll admit he's made a mistake and say he's truly sorry, but that doesn't make it hurt any less.

"Just say it," I cut him off. "Admit that me…us…was an error in judgement that you'll never revisit again."

"You think this is painless for me? I told you how I feel about you. It doesn't get any easier when we're together. But I can put my feelings aside and promise you a strong working relationship."

Heat rises to my cheeks at how unfair this has ended, with him getting everything that's important to him and me only the job I want.

"You need me to be your work spouse, is that it? That's the only value I have? To make sure that Councilman Bennett has a brilliant career at City Hall so he can eventually move on to play politics with the big boys?" And leave Chloe behind for another work spouse who's willing to be his steppingstone.

For a moment, his lips press into a sad line. "I'd like to be your work spouse," he says. "You know it goes both ways. I'll support your career too, if you'll let me. That's my value to you. You're right; if I'm successful here, I will move on and I want you with me."

For him, it's settled. I don't care about the sweet fucking by and by. It's the promise I made to the mayor I have to live through, if I want to be Assistant City Manager. If I'm going to work on his team, I need to hear him say why we can't be together. I need him to say it's Pamela he loves. I want his words to cut so deep that the pain kills this love for him that's kept me a prisoner.

"Why, Jax?" I demand. "Why won't you let us happen? I love you."

He stills as another of my guarded secrets escapes into the world, and I catch his stunned face before I pivot away from embarrassment. How stupid to blurt out my feelings as if that will change reality. Now he's convinced I'm one of his lovesick supporters. This is not an infatuation I feel for him; it's like a borderline sickness, it's so real. His arms come around me from behind, pulling me to him. I feel safe enveloped in his strength. This is where I've always belonged with him. He kisses my hair and an emotional surge warms me with hope.

"It's okay," he soothes. "We'll sort it out and it'll be alright."

Hope falls when I realize he's not saying our love will get us through this.

"It will never be alright." I ease myself from his embrace to face him. "Tell me why, Jax. Stop this goddamn procrastination and tell me why we can't start over."

He hesitates while he searches for a way to say what I don't want to hear. He reaches out for me, but I avoid his touch.

"We need to settle this now," I warn. "Touching me will only give me false hope. Say it."

His jaw tightens as surprise turns into frustration that this tactic won't work. "I'm your boss, okay? It's a potential scandal. It could impede our careers."

"Our careers have nothing to do with it."

"Ivarsson, I've already explained that I'm not willing to let you throw your reputation away. The press can be brutal about stuff like this, especially to the woman. Think about it—if this doesn't work out between us, you'll end up hating me for more than a broken heart, if it comes to that."

I'm willing to take a chance if things were different. If he won't admit the real reason, I will. "I know you're hiding something."

Our voices might be projecting a little too loudly. I'm aware of two people skirting by us with curious glances. Jax pretends interest in a shop window, keeping his face away from foot traffic while I give a couple an awkward smile.

"This place is too public to have this discussion. We need to leave," I suggest, "before someone recognizes you and the camera phones come out."

"You're right." He grabs my hand, pulling me along to the car. I let him lead me because I'm just as eager to leave. We enter the car, slamming the doors too hard. Jax puts the Jag in gear and tears out of the lot like we're leaving the scene of a crime. We travel in silence as he maneuvers the sports car through back streets until he pulls into the lot of a closed warehouse and kills the engine. He looks at me, resigned. "Go ahead, get it all out so we can settle this."

I'm not happy that he seems to think I'm the problem. I ignore his direction and take a breath to calm the adrenaline that's threatening to push my heart out of my chest. "We've been together for days. Why didn't you mention you were engaged to Pamela?"

He glances over the steering wheel. "Who told you Bruce and I are engaged?"

"Jessica. She told me yesterday after I met Pamela. After she left us to run errands. She said you met at Princeton and have been together ever since."

He shakes his head. "It's true we met at school, but we're not engaged."

I sink back into the seat, ready for another round of half-truths. "Why would your mother tell me something I could easily confirm? Don't tell me she hates me that much to tell me a lie for short-term pleasure?"

"Because we were, but we're not now. We haven't told Mother yet."

I take a few moments to process what he just said. "When did the engagement end?"

"About three weeks ago. It's been over for a long time. We didn't tell my mother because she was looking forward to our wedding, and we were waiting for the right moment."

He can't look at me while he conveys the information, preventing me from understanding what this broken engagement means to him.

"I thought we would give her the news when I lost the election. You know, throwing one more piece of bad news onto another, but that didn't happen."

"Then what were the two of you talking about when I arrived, and why was Jessica snippy with me today?"

Jax rubs his temples, hesitating. "I told her we postponed the wedding because of my work at City Hall and Bruce wants to start a graduate program at Stanford. She didn't believe me. She thinks the wedding is on hold because I'm interested in you."

Jessica saw the attraction and didn't want him to throw his future away on me. "What did you say to her?"

He takes a breath. "I had to tell her something before it got worse. I didn't want her to confront you, but now I see it was too late."

"What did you tell her?" I whisper.

"I told her there's nothing between us and that it's Pamela Bruce I'm spending the rest of my life with."

My phone pings. I pull my cell from my bag and read the message. "Good news," I say without happiness. "I'll stay on your team. Please take me to my car."

20

Baby Come Back

Jax pulls into his parking space at City Hall. He says nothing when I push out and take my anger out on slamming the door. I imagine he's watching me stomp away to the less-privileged employee parking lot, because I don't look back.

It's comforting driving in the ebb and flow of the city streets while I think. The Assistant City Manager position fell into my lap for a price; I just need to wait until the current occupant of that position leaves sometime next year. I have to put up with a man who won't break his stupid code of dating someone he manages and if I leave his team, I forfeit a job I've wanted all my life.

This present situation stems from one night, one event, a teenage heartbreak that holds me in limbo. My regret is that I didn't fight for Jax the first time he left me behind. When he didn't return and there was no contact, I spiraled down into my sorrow. If I accept this now, I'll never move on. I'll be in this pathetic state forever.

The tires screech when I make a U-turn, evoking the honking

wrath of a few drivers. I don't care; I need to find the only person who can help me. It's getting dark, but there's always someone at a fire station, as long as they're not out on a call.

Tyler is there at the desk and, based on his toothy grin, he remembers me. "Hey, Chloe, did you come for another tour?" he teases.

"No," I say with a chuckle. "I think I can walk this place blindfolded. I stopped by to see Brody; is he around?"

"Brody's off today, and he won't be back on for a few days. Can I help you with something?"

"I was running an errand down the street and thought I'd say hi. No problem, I'll catch him next time." I head for the door.

"You should call him," he shouts after me.

"Yeah, that's a good idea. Thanks," I say over my shoulder.

My keys jangle as I push them into the ignition. I don't have the energy to start the engine, so I sit back to watch the sluggish line of rush hour traffic make its way down the street. Calling Brody would be a great idea if I had his number. I can't wait for a few days for Brody to appear at work. I have an idea that might work.

Walking through the door of the Brute Force gym, I'm confronted by the sound of exertion and the familiar scent of old sweat. There's a class standing at ringside. About ten people, gloved and wearing protective headgear, are watching a grizzled, gray-haired instructor correcting a student's stance.

I scan the packed gym for Brody's tousled black hair, but all I get are curious glances. I'm chewing my bottom lip, doubting my plan.

"Chloe." My name flies out from the back of the gym. Lindy is moving through the patrons toward me. "Did you come about the women's class? You missed the last one; that was on Wednesday." She's moving past me. "Come with me to the office and I'll sign you up." I follow her inside the room that hasn't seen a cleaning crew for ages. She steps behind a desk piled with papers, a laptop, and a water bottle.

She moves stacks of papers around, looking for something.

"I know I have a sign-up form here. But if you want to do this online, we can do this through the website. Here, have a seat."

I plop into a chair in front of the desk, watching her hunt for the form.

"I found it!" she says, raising the paper up. "You can use your phone instead, but this might be faster." She hands me the form. "I'll make a copy of what you fill out. It can be your receipt and there's a list of equipment you'll need before your first class on there. Lucky for you, you can buy whatever you need here in our equipment boutique."

I search the paper, staring at the words, trying to figure out how to tell her I'm not here for the women's boxing class. I place the form on her desk. "Thanks, Lindy, but I'm not here to sign up for the class."

She sits hard in her seat and leans back, wary. "Did you want another punching lesson? I can do that. I'm actually better at the bag than Brody."

"I have no doubt that's true," I say with a smile. "But I'm here because I was hoping to catch Brody. I need to talk to him."

Lindy looks out through the large window that affords her a view of her bustling gym. "You might see him tonight, but he hasn't been here since he brought you to the gym. For a while there I thought he stopped coming."

"I wouldn't normally ask, but can you give me his phone number? I've already stopped by the fire station. He's not working today and won't be back for a few days."

Her chair squeaks as she thinks. "Brody doesn't pick up the phone if he doesn't recognize the number. He's kind of a dick that way. You'll have to go over to his place. I don't know what you'll find when you get over there. I've never been to his apartment."

That was cryptic, and her face doesn't tell me anything. "Do you mean he might be with a female?"

She shrugs. "He might be with a goat, for all I know. We've

known each other for a long time, but I know little about his personal life. You're the only woman I've seen him with."

I hadn't thought he might be seeing someone or maybe living with a girlfriend. This must be a friendly warning to be careful with Brody. "I'm willing to take a chance," I say. "I'd appreciate your help."

Her fingers make a few quick taps on the desk. "There's the matter of privacy. He's a member of Brute Force, and if I give out his address, it could be a breach of trust."

"So you're saying no?"

"I didn't say that."

I'm surprised, but I understand her meaning. This is a monetary exchange. "Okay, how much money do you want for the address?"

She gives a slight tilt to her head, a slow smile reaching across her lips. "I've said nothing about money."

This is getting interesting. Besides money, what could she want from me? I lean back, cross my legs, and wait for her to reveal her price.

She knows she has the advantage because that half-smile hasn't left her face. "You can have the address and I'll even throw in directions if you'll attend one complimentary session of the women's boxing class."

I didn't see that coming and I almost laugh out of relief, but it's still an unusual request.

"Why is it important for me to attend your boxing class? You've got a packed gym; it doesn't look like you're hurting for customers."

She moves forward, elbows on the desk. "Have you ever heard the concept of a loss leader?"

"Yeah, where a store offers a ridiculously low price for an item to lure people in. Like selling twenty-pound turkeys for a dollar during Thanksgiving. The customer gets the cheap turkey but ends up spending a couple hundred dollars for all the sides on top of their regular shopping."

"You know the concept. Well, I see you as a loss leader. I'm hoping if someone like you likes the class, you'll tell your friends about it."

"Like me?"

"Yeah, the lipstick, nail polish, upwardly mobile, trendy bitches."

"A-l-r-i-g-h-t," I say, drawing out the word, while I imagine facing someone in a boxing ring.

"Look." She pulls a flyer from her desk drawer and does a two-finger slide of the paper across to me. "The purpose of the class is not to beat you bloody. We don't do hard contact. It's cardio, self-defense, and helps with self-esteem."

I'm still not convinced. The most aggressive physical contact I've had is a pillow fight.

"Don't worry, you'll still look pretty after your class. Did I mention they're a great bunch of women, and it's always good to expand your circle of friends, right?"

I nod, retrieving the flyer from her desk, careful not to laugh. Now I see why Brody likes her. "Deal." I push the paper into my purse and retrieve my phone. "Here," I say as I hand the cell to her, "or would you prefer writing the information on the back of the flyer?"

Lindy walks me out to my car at the front of the building. We watch the headlights from a few cars travel down the street, but no one stops. Nothing looks occupied on this block except for Brute Force, so my guess is that they're passing through to other destinations. Standing outside in the dark with only a dim glow from the gym for light, it feels desolate in this area.

"Brody's a good guy," she says, glancing past me down the street. "If he calls you a friend, he's with you for life."

I nod, wondering if she saw me agreeing with her in this light.

She leans against my car, arms folded. "Those loft apartments he's in are not far from here. My dad and I own that one and a few other warehouse apartment buildings. When Dad found out Brody was a firefighter, he gave him the apartment at a ridiculously low rent. It's a way for him to give back to first responders."

I take a spot next to her, looking back at the gym. "I'm sure he appreciates the help."

"We've done that with a few other units for people who have jobs in Silicon Valley but can't afford the high rents. I only wish we could do more."

She pushes to her feet, signaling an end to our discussion. I do the same. I need to see Brody and she has a gym to run.

"Thanks for the help, Lindy." I put my arms around her for a hug and she reciprocates, holding me tight.

"Come to the class when you have the time; there's no pressure. It will be good to see you again."

Lindy gave me the code to get through the security gate to the parking lot complex. I find the second set of codes on my phone and punch it into the keypad to enter the building. The plaque outside says they built this warehouse in 1920. They converted it into five floors of apartments about fifteen years ago.

Brody lives on the top floor of this trendy residence. I pass up the elevator for the open stairwell in the middle of the building to help me calm my nervous stomach. There are large windows on either end of the building that flood the stairs and corridors with natural light during the day. Music drifts from the 5th floor as I approach the top landing of the stairs. The hallway appears to vibrate. I find my pace matching the music while I looked for apartment 505.

The song providing the raucous concert is Missio's Temple Priest. Music pulsates from his apartment; I imagine everything inside is vibrating with sound.

I knock, but how can he hear me with the music blaring? I use my fist and bang on the door with part frustration from my lunch with Jax and part from my need to be heard. It works; there's dead silence, but nothing else. I raise my fist for another round of pounding when the door flies open.

"For fuck's sake, Cole, it's not even 9 o'clock. I can play my music…" He glances down at me. It hasn't fully registered what he's seeing yet.

"You're not Cole."

I'm staring at a bare-chested Brody, and a sheen of sweat glistens his body. "No, I'm not."

He takes a step out into the hall for a quick look, then pulls me inside. He walks across the room to a weight bench and grabs a T-shirt. Pulling it over his head, I'm staring at rock-hard abs until his head pops through the opening and the show is over. "How did you find me?" he asks, padding barefoot across the room.

"Lindy gave me your address. She said you wouldn't pick up if you didn't know it was my number."

"Yeah, she says I'm a dick for not answering my phone if I don't know who it is. I'm not wasting my time with telemarketers."

"She told me."

"Why are you here? Did something happen?"

"I need your help."

"Why?"

Before I can answer, he holds up his hand to halt the conversation, "Never mind. I stink. Let me shower first, then we can talk."

He moves further into the space, pulling off his shirt. "There's wine and beer in the fridge…help yourself."

I crane my neck to see the last of that really fine ass turn the corner.

21

Rescue Me

I pull out a beer from the fridge, pop the top, and take a long drag. I run my fingers along the black countertop as I walk out of the kitchen area. The place is neat; I mean *everything in its place wiped clean* neat. It's a big, open industrial space with a lot of the original structure intact. I love these reclamation projects that preserve and modernize buildings for a new use.

The polished concrete floor is a variegated deep bronze. It's probably cold in the early morning before the heat kicks in and cool in the summer. I stand in the middle of the space, admiring the track lighting that softens the exposed brick and doesn't spoil the view through the massive rolled-steel windows that take up three sides.

Furniture defines the living areas. A heavy, dark-wood table and chairs for the dining section. Two mustard couches and a few scattered tables for the living room with a huge TV suspended from the ceiling. It's a large space for one person. If I didn't know someone lived here, I'd say they staged this place for a home tour.

The only enclosed area is the bathroom on the other side of the kitchen. Across from this is a mini gym with a full set of weights, bench, treadmill, and heavy bag. I give a wide path to the bathroom to see the rest of the loft. A large, burnished-metal divider, that looks like it doubles as an art piece, separates his bedroom from the rest of the area. I'm about to step around the barrier when the water stops. I turn away from his bedroom and head back to the kitchen.

Brody appears moments later in a black T-shirt, sweats, and still no shoes. He walks by, finger-combing his dark hair, leaving the scent of soap in his wake. He reaches in the fridge and pulls out a beer.

"I had you figured for a wine and Brie snob."

I nearly cough up my beer. "Yeah, well, looks can be deceiving."

He leans against the counter. "You hungry?" He takes a drink.

I watched Jax eat his late lunch, so I'm ready for food. "Yes, would you like to go to a restaurant? I don't know this area, but I can find something through my restaurant app."

He lets out a guffaw. "I'm offering to cook."

I forgot he's a firehouse cook. "Sure, that would be great. Can I help?"

"You can make the salad." Moving to the fridge, he extracts the lettuce. "Have you ever made salad dressing from scratch?"

If he wants me to warm up some toaster pastry, I'm his girl. I'm sure I'm giving him the deer-in-the-headlights look.

"Well, I guess that would be a no." He pulls out more salad stuff.

After a five-minute lesson on how to make dressing and how to properly assemble a salad, Brody ties on an apron, fills a huge pot from the tap, sets it on the stove, and dumps a ton of salt in the water.

Thirty minutes later, we're at the table. He's opening a bottle of wine while I'm placing pasta on my plate and marveling that I made salad dressing.

I watched him sauté garlic, mushrooms, and make some kind of sauce with pasta water and cheese. After he added the cooked pasta, he finished with torn pieces of a thin Italian ham and parsley. It seems close to magic to me.

He watches as I take my first bite. The pasta tastes like heaven. I put my fork down and cover my mouth so he can't see me chewing. "Brody, this is restaurant quality. I never thought—"

"That I can cook something other than chili and ribs?" He shakes his head at me underestimating him again. "Those guys at the fire station have sophisticated tastes." He pulls the cork and glances at me while filling my glass and smiles with genuine pride.

I get a flashback of him tying on his apron. I realize this kitchen is where he did his photo shoot for the calendar. I'm having a hard time getting that image out of my mind, along with how he looked when he opened the door. I drop my hand to rummage in my bag for my phone. I pull it out and snap a picture.

"Hey." He gives me a half-hearted protest. "I thought we were past that?"

"You gave me permission to photograph you until I feel safe, remember? I'm still not sure about you, Brody Knox."

I check the photo. The camera loves him, even in an old T-shirt and sweats. I haven't taken any shots since we were at Brute Force. I'm swiping through his pictures, surprised I caught so many of his moods.

He thrusts out his hand. "Let me have the phone."

I reluctantly give it to him. "Please stand," he asks. I'm up and he moves from his chair to stand next to me. His arm is around me, crushing me to his chest. He raises the phone above us. "Say garlic," he says and snaps a selfie. "One more look at the camera." I do as he turns towards me and snaps another. Brody taps on my phone. "I'm going to give you my phone number, so at least you don't think I'm a dick. I've sent those pictures to my phone…what's your number?" I rattle it off and he pushes send.

We continue dinner talking about general topics. Brody doesn't ask why I'm here, and at this point I don't want to offer. I'm enjoying this meal and his company. We finish after an hour and I trail behind him with plates to the kitchen, helping him to rinse and load the dishwasher. He picks up the wine bottle from dinner and squints at it. "Looks like there's half left. Let's sit on the couch and finish this off."

I sit facing him on the opposite couch. Brody motions with the bottle to hold out my glass. He tops mine and his, then places it on the coffee table. "I think it's time you tell me why you're here."

I'm already relaxed from the wine at dinner, but Brody's expectant face has me back on my mission. I take a breath. "I want you to marry me, and how do you feel about getting me pregnant immediately?" I blurt out.

Surprise widens Brody's eyes, then he shoots up from the couch, a little unsteady. "I think we need another bottle," he mumbles, walking toward the kitchen.

"It's not as dire as all that," I say to his back. "None of it will be real. If I'm going to make Jax jealous, I need more than a pretend boyfriend, I need someone who wants to be my husband."

He comes back with an open bottle. "It's a start. I think I know a couple guys that will want to be your boyfriend or fiancée. What's your plan?"

I put my glass down. "You said you'd help."

"Yes, I did, but I never promised to be the boyfriend. I think Tyler would work. He asked about you the day you were at the station. I know he's interested."

"I like Tyler, but I don't need a lovesick recruit fawning all over me. I can find one of those at the city."

Brody's brows go up. "Been pushing up the temperature of those young interns at the city?" he teases.

"Brody, I need you to help me. Jax will hate that we're together. I thought you could ask me to marry you at the office or some other public place, or maybe at a council meeting. I have to attend those."

"Trust me, that won't work."

"Why?"

Brody towers over me, and it forces me to sit back and look up at him. He gestures with the bottle. "If I come in, out of the blue, and ask you to marry me, he'll see that stench a mile out. You'll look desperate and you've lost your shot."

I thought I had the perfect plan and the guy to help me. I slip off my heels and tuck my legs to the side, the top half of me on the armrest. I grab my wine, knock it back, and hold out my glass for a refill. "Okay, what do you suggest?"

Brody lands next to me on the couch. "Let him see the first meeting where the sparks fly…and the pursuit. He's got to see someone has a growing interest in you, so you can stoke that jealousy fire. I'm not your guy. I'll give you my advice, but that's it."

I'm so close to getting Jax, I've got the job I want, and if Brody changes his mind and helps me, I'll have everything. Then my conversation with Lindy flashes in my mind.

"What do you want?"

He slips his gaze over to me. "What do you mean?"

"What do you want to play the part of the man who's crazy in love with me? There must be something you want; I can pay you."

"You can't afford me," he laughs and takes a drink.

"I'm a trust fund kid who has control of her funds."

He glances at me to check if this is a joke.

I'm not smiling.

"It's true, I am," I say. Then something dawns on me. "You mentioned you're interested in the paramedic program, but you can't afford the course. The fire department is my area of expertise." I search my brain for the requirements on paramedics. I snap my fingers. "Officially, the requirements state they will take applicants that have completed the paramedic course, but quietly they want firefighters with a four-year degree and completion of the paramedic program. Brody, I can pay for all of it hundreds of times over."

"No." The refusal resonates deep in his throat.

"Help me and walk away with something you want. I'll get the satisfaction of knowing we have another skilled medical professional for the community. We'll all get what we want."

He's shutting down, not making eye contact. "I'm not interested."

I plow on, determine to change his mind. "Even if your goal is to be a nurse or doctor, I'll do it. Tell me what you want."

He gets up, snatching the half-empty bottle from the table, and heads to the kitchen.

I follow him. He stops in the middle of his kitchen with his back to me.

I'm going to screw this up and lose him too. How would I feel if someone I barely knew started throwing money at me?

I want to place my hand on his back, but I resist the urge and keep my distance.

"I'm sorry if I offended you," I say, meaning the apology. "I got excited that I could help you get your dream, like you're helping me get mine. I just need you to hear my proposal and then you can decide."

He doesn't object, so I go on. "I'll set up an account under your name. Once the money is there, it's yours; do whatever you want with the money. There will be enough for you to get a four-year degree, medical school, your residency, and all other expenses while you're working to be a doctor; a full ride. This is your chance to do what you've always dreamed of: to practice medicine. I'd like to be the first to call you Dr. Knox."

I take a step closer, gambling I won't hear a real 'no.' "Keep the money if this plan doesn't work out; at least I'll be happy that something positive came of it."

His silent, tense body is still facing away, his fingers tight around the neck of the bottle.

I inch forward until I'm a breath away from his broad back. His muscles bunch when I place a light hand on his back, but he doesn't shy away from my touch.

"Brody, do you want me on my knees?" I whisper. "Because I'll do it; I'll beg."

Author's Note

Thank you for reading Work Spouse, which is book 1 of a 2-book mini-series. The story continues with Work with Me; out April 2021 and is the conclusion of this story.

The Love@work series was planned as five stand-alone novels. Best laid plans...right?

I think the series is a bit unusual because the first book of the series, *Trinal*, is an erotic novella which makes it different from the other full-length novels, but the story is still in the realm of the world I created for this series. In fact, some of the story from *Trinal* trickles into *Work Spouse* (couldn't help it…it just happened). So, if you've read the series from the beginning, you'll catch the references.

Never having written a series before, I thought all the books would be self-contained stand-alones. That intention held until *Work Spouse*, which has several characters from *Love Contract* making an appearance.

When I wrote *Work Spouse*, maybe it was the inclusion of previous characters that grew the book into two. So, when we end on a cliffhanger in *Work Spouse*, we finish up with *Work with Me*, which will be available April 2021.

Characters from both *Love Contract* and *Work Spouse* show up in *Queen Bee*, which will be the last novel in the series. Stay tuned for my announcement about when *Queen Bee* will release. If you want to be notified, sign up for my newsletter, Pax World, or follow me on Amazon or BookBub, and you won't miss the announcement.

When Love@work is completed, we go into the world of wine and

Scotsmen. Trust me, it's a great pairing. Yeah, I know, stupid pun. Even though it will be big men in kilts drinking wine, it still stays in Silicon Valley

Special Note About Reviews

If you liked *Work Spouse*, please leave a review or give me a shout-out on social media. Just click any or all of the links below if you have the ebook. If you have the paperback, head on over to Amazon or to the other sites below to leave your review. Your honest opinion is important!

Amazon | Goodreads | BookBub

Another Way to Leave a Review

For those of you who break out in hives when you have to write something or don't want to navigate Amazon, Goodreads or Bookbub's review system. Just leave a rating at the end of this ebook without a review for Amazon.

Your rating will be added to the book's star ratings and will be much, much appreciated.

If you have the paperback book, you'll need to go on the site to do the same....sorry.

If you're thinking about how many stars to leave, I'd suggest 5 stars, but that's just me.

About the Author

Pax Sinclair is a contemporary romance novelist who writes about the steamy, sexy side of the high-power tech world of Silicon Valley. Sure, her stories are about billionaire tech moguls, but you'll also meet other characters that make the valley sizzle.

Come along for a ride in Pax World where it's always funny, quirky, steamy and sometimes erotic.

Pax lives and works in Silicon Valley. She's a California native.

BEFORE YOU GO

Join my mailing list to receive my monthly newsletter, PaxWorld. Keep up-to-day on upcoming books, read excepts, enter contests and give-aways. You'll also find free and discounted romance ebooks to download from my author friends. (You can easily unsubscribe at any time) Visit https://www.subscribepage.com/paxworld to sign-up for the PaxWorld newsletter.

Visit Me
paxsinclair.com, Goodreads, Amazon Author Central, BookBub, Facebook, Instagram

Love@work Series
Trinal – Book 1 (Available now on Amazon)
Love Contract – Book 2 (Available now on Amazon)
Work Spouse – Book 3 (Available now on Amazon)
Work with Me – Book 4 (Coming April 2021)
Queen Bee – Book 5

YOU MIGHT ALSO ENJOY

Sweet and Sultry Series
Someone Like You - Book 1 (Available now on Amazon)

www.ingramcontent.com/pod-product-compliance
Lightning Source LLC
Chambersburg PA
CBHW032007240626
47153CB00003B/1154